ANN BARKER

CLERKENWELL CONSPIRACY

Complete and Unabridged

ULVERSCROFT
Leicester

First published in Great Britain in 2008 by
Robert Hale Limited
London

First Large Print Edition
published 2008
by arrangement with
Robert Hale Limited
London

British Library CIP Data

Barker, Ann
  Clerkenwell conspiracy.—Large print ed.—
  Ulverscroft large print series: adventure & suspense
  1. Widows—Fiction 2. Bookstores—Fiction
  3. Clerkenwell (London, England)—Fiction
  4. Love stories 5. Large type books
  I. Title
  823.9′2 [F]

  ISBN 978–1–84782–476–9

Published by
F. A. Thorpe (Publishing)
Anstey, Leicestershire
Set by Words & Graphics Ltd.
Anstey, Leicestershire
Printed and bound in Great Britain by
T. J. International Ltd., Padstow, Cornwall

This book is printed on acid-free paper

*To Jonathan and all those he cares
about: love, always.*

1

'At last! How long can it possibly take to fetch a shawl, for God's sake?' Mrs Comberton took the shawl handed to her without a word of thanks. 'I suppose you've been dallying in the nursery again,' she added querulously. 'Upon my soul, I don't know what you think I — ' she broke off, recalling that she did not in fact pay the woman standing in front of her: — 'house you for,' she concluded.

'No, I haven't been to the nursery,' the other replied in a reasonable tone, prudently ignoring most of this ungracious speech. 'Your maid could not find the shawl you wanted straight away.'

'You will be saying next that that is *my* fault,' answered Mrs Comberton defensively. 'Oh never mind, never mind. Just go to the desk and get out a pen. I am going to give a dinner party, and I want you to make a list of the names of the people that I mean to invite. Then you may write out the invitations. It is very important that this dinner should go well, because Bunty is back!'

As far as Eve Scorer was concerned, this

last piece of information was unwelcome in the extreme. A year living with her cousin had taught her better than to show any reaction, however, so she said nothing in response, but walked over to the desk in the window, sat down gracefully, took up a pen and prepared to write. Not that she really needed to hear the list which her cousin would dictate. She knew the names from which the selection would be made, and could make a fair guess as to which people would be favoured with an invitation. Why Julia always had to make such a performance of this activity was a mystery to her. The only reason that occurred to her was that she enjoyed playing the part of *grande dame*, acting as hostess to the neighbours, impressing them with the quality of her china and the food served thereon, and ensuring happiness or chagrin by the conferring or withholding of an invitation.

This was partly true. The widow of the Honourable Neville Comberton, younger son of the Earl of Wirksworth, Julia undoubtedly had an entrée to the highest circles that society could offer. However, Eve also suspected that because Julia was so idle, she was obliged to stretch out activities such as the present one in order to fill her otherwise empty days.

'I think that I must invite General Sparrow

and his daughter,' Julia began.

'General Sparrow and Miss Sparrow,' Eve said obediently. She had already written the names down. She looked outside. The sun was shining and the garden looked very inviting. Perhaps she would have time to take the children out later.

'Sir Laurence and Lady Buckles ought to come,' Julia said next.

These names, also, Eve had written down. The next few on the list would prove problematical, she knew, so she waited for Julia to make her decision.

'Now, we had Mr and Mrs Bunty last time, but only under sufferance, because I always think that Mrs Bunty smells of the shop, but we can hardly have Horace without his parents, or even without their other tedious son, so we will have to have them all. Perhaps we ought to have the vicar and his wife and their plain daughter. After all, Mrs Plover's father is a baronet, as she never ceases to tell everyone.' She paused, then said, 'No, cross them out. Plover was quite offensive in the sermon that he preached last week. 'Blessed are the poor' indeed! Where upon earth can he have got that idea from?' Nobly refraining from saying 'the Bible', Eve remained prudently silent with pen in hand.

There was another pause. 'Wait, though. If

3

we cross out the vicar and his wife, we can hardly have the Misses Hardiment, since they are related to the vicar and will wonder why he is not there. We must have the Misses Hardiment, since they are very good friends of the Duke of Honiton, and if they should ever have him to stay, or dine, it would be a disaster if we were not invited; so put them down.'

Again Eve waited, pen in hand. She was under no illusions that the word 'we' included herself. It was more in the nature of a royal 'we', she thought wryly.

'No, on second thoughts, don't put them down, because if we have them, we shall be too many ladies.' Another long pause. 'Wait; will Sir Laurence and Lady Buckles be able to come? After all, Lady Buckles has not long finished lying-in.'

'I think, ma'am, that she is now beginning to get about again,' Eve ventured.

'*Is* she? Well I must say, I think that it is about time that she did so. Such a fuss she made over having that baby. I cannot understand why people have to make such a to-do over what is after all a very simple procedure.'

Knowing that whereas her cousin had indeed given birth to a son two years before with the utmost ease, Lady Buckles, by way of contrast, had had a very difficult labour which had nearly taken her life, Eve made no response to this.

'Well, I shall invite them, and if she cannot come, then you will have to take her place. You will then have the pleasure of having Horace Bunty dance attendance upon you.'

'Thank you, Cousin, I am obliged to you,' Eve replied with an irony that quite escaped her relative. 'I am far from aspiring to the dizzy heights of Mr Bunty's approval, however.'

'Don't try to pull the wool over my eyes, miss,' said Julia sharply. 'I have seen you making sheep's eyes at him.'

'I have been doing no such thing, and I am not 'miss',' answered Eve, just as sharply.

Realizing that she had gone too far, Julia looked down, fidgetting with her hand-kerchief. 'I know you are only trying to find excuses for not helping me,' she said, pouting. 'I am sure my friend Mrs Sallis has said so a good many times. 'You have taken that young woman in virtually off the street', she has told me. 'She cannot expect to sit twiddling her thumbs'.'

Sternly repressing the urge to turn round and hurl the ink pot at her insensitive kinswoman, Eve merely murmured, 'Just so, ma'am. Have you decided upon your final list for the party?'

Mrs Comberton leaned back, closing her eyes. 'Oh, I don't know,' she said wearily. 'Invite them all and let them fight it out when they get here. I am far too exhausted to worry about it. I had the most wretched night. I think I shall go and lie down whilst you finish the list and write the invitations.'

'Very well, ma'am,' Eve answered. If her cousin actually did anything during the day, she might feel more ready for sleep at night, she reflected, as she took up her pen again, and turned her mind to the task in hand.

Eve Scorer had been living with her cousin at Stonecrop Manor for just over a year, from shortly after the death of her husband in the Egyptian campaign in 1801, when he had been serving as a captain of dragoons under General Abercrombie.

Eve was the only child of Hubert and Maud Colby, both of whom had made what had been considered to be an unwise marriage, and had therefore been cut off by their respective families. Her mother had died some years before, and she and her father had just about managed on his small annuity. Eve and Edmund Scorer had been childhood sweethearts, living in the same village where Edmund's father was the vicar. Like Eve,

Edmund was an only child and the two had played together as children, before friendship had grown into love.

Edmund had always had his heart set upon joining the army, and with considerable self-sacrifice, his parents had purchased his commission. He and Eve had married shortly before he had sailed to the West Indies with his regiment and, as Eve's father died at about this time, and his annuity died with him, Eve went to live with Edmund's parents.

There was not very much to go round, and they were dependent partly upon Mr Scorer's stipend and partly upon the money that Edmund was able to send home. Eve's discovery that she was with child was a cause for rejoicing, although an anxiety as well, but they managed to keep cheerful. The time that Edmund was able to spend at home with them just after baby Luke was born was particularly joyful.

The Revd Samuel Scorer had not lived for long after the birth of his grandson, and times were hard for the little family. Promotion for the young army officer meant that he was able to send a little more home. By dint of growing their own vegetables and by Eve's doing a little teaching in the village school while Luke remained with his grandmother, they were able to manage, living in a cottage which a local landowner was prepared to let them have at a very small charge out of respect for Edmund's father. It was a quiet, peaceful existence, which suited Mrs Scorer senior very well, but Eve often felt bored nearly to screaming point. She would have liked nothing better than to have followed the drum, but the nature of Edmund's appointment in the West Indies had made this inappropriate, and once her mother-in-law was widowed, she could not be left. Eve often wondered whether she would ever be allowed to do anything more exciting than stay at home in the quiet village in which they lived.

When Luke was nearly five, her life took a different turn in the most undesirable way possible. She received a letter to tell her that her husband, Captain Edmund Scorer, had been killed in action. She tried to break the news gently to her mother-in-law, but the shock was too great. Just two days after hearing these dreadful tidings, Mrs Scorer died of a heart attack.

It was not without a great deal of heart-searching that Eve decided to apply to her cousin for help. The two women were very much of an age, and had married within a few months of each other. There the similarity had ended, for whereas Eve had married her childhood sweetheart, Julia had set her heart on wealth and position, eventually marrying the younger son of an earl. Eve knew that she would not find her cousin congenial company, but she had little choice in the matter. Until Luke was older, she could not hope to find paid employment, and his needs had to come first. She did receive a little from the army, but she was determined to put this on one side for Luke's education in future years.

With all this in mind, she had written to her cousin asking for assistance. Julia had written back to say that, as she had recently been widowed herself, Eve could come to live with them and make herself useful. Eve had accepted this rather ungracious offer, and had soon found that Mrs Comberton's definition of usefulness was remarkably broad. It included all the aspects of caring for a household that were not to Julia's liking, such as conferring with the housekeeper to make sure that all was running smoothly, inspecting the linen and the still room, and discussing menus with the cook. It also included visiting local families, collecting items from the village shop, and cutting and arranging flowers, in addition to organizing the nursery, which housed young Master Comberton, as well as Luke. Finally and, Eve suspected most importantly, it included running after Mrs

Comberton, fetching and carrying for her and anticipating her every possible want. As for twiddling her thumbs, chance would be a fine thing.

The invitations completed, Eve went upstairs. The day was still fine, and the children would benefit from some fresh air. One of the advantages of Julia's indolence was that she never interfered in the nursery. This meant that Eve more or less had a free hand in organizing the care of her son and her nephew. Both Luke and his cousin showed their delight at her arrival, Luke by exclaiming 'Mama!' and running to receive her embrace, and Thomas by tottering over more slowly, gurgling 'Teeve, Teeve,' which was the nearest to 'Aunt Eve' that he could manage. It did not take long to prepare the children for going outside — nurse, who approved heartily of Mrs Scorer, having agreed to the scheme — and very soon, Eve, Thomas, Luke, and Polly, the nursery maid, were outside playing a game of ball. Thomas, still in skirts as was appropriate for his babyhood, staggered about, fell over, laughed, and barely joined in the game. Luke, however, wearing his first nankeen breeches, and very conscious of his seniority, paid careful attention and took part with keen enjoyment tempered with seriousness.

It was at such times that he looked most like his father, and Eve found herself regretting most profoundly that Luke would never know him. He would, however, know a good deal about him. On Edmund's death, Eve had received a most compassionate letter from her husband's commanding officer. She had read it so often that she knew it by heart.

Madam

It is with much regret that I write to inform you of the death of your husband, Captain Scorer. He was a fine officer, whose devotion to duty was exemplary, and he will be sorely missed by officers and men alike. When I return to England, I will do myself the honour of calling upon you to give you his possessions, including his sword, which he carried with so much distinction. In the meantime, I would be very glad if you will tell me if I may serve you in any way.

I understand that you have a young son. Captain Scorer spoke to me of him and of yourself with great affection. That your son should grow to be as gallant a gentleman as his father is the sincere wish of

Your humble and obedient servant,

Jason Ballantyne
Colonel of Dragoons

It had been over a year now, and the colonel had not yet called, but Eve knew that he had been on active service. Doubtless he had barely been in England for long enough to attend to any personal matters, let alone pay visits to distant parts of the country. The letter she had put away carefully so that she could show it to Luke when he was old enough. The sword, too, would belong to him when he grew up.

From Edmund's letters it had been clear that he and his men had idolized 'Colonel Blazes' as he was known. The tales of his courage and compassion had peppered the letters that Edmund had sent home, until Eve had been filled with a longing to meet the man, not simply to hear the colonel's recollections of her late husband, but to discover whether the folklore that clung to him was grounded in any reality.

Her gaze rested on the other child. Lord Wirksworth's heir, Viscount Bradwell, was a naval captain, and had distinguished himself in a number of engagements. He was as yet unmarried, so the hopes of the succession rested with this young child. The Earl of Wirksworth, although not entirely happy about this state of affairs, was prepared to tolerate it. This was partly because theirs was a family with a long and distinguished naval tradition, going back to the days of Queen Elizabeth, when a Comberton had served under Drake, thereby earning elevation to the peerage to become the first earl.

Eve knew from things that Julia had let slip from time to time that her cousin secretly entertained the hope that her brother-in-law would be killed in action, so that her son might eventually become the earl. In the meantime, however, she played the part of the dutiful sister-in-law, sending Captain Lord Bradwell regular attentive letters, doubtless with the hope that if he survived the action in the current war, he would remember her kindness and show his gratitude by making sure that she received plenty of invitations to Wirksworth Hall.

2

As it turned out, Eve was obliged to attend her cousin's dinner party. This was because Julia had decided to receive the vicar after all and, as his brother was visiting him from Oxford, she felt bound to invite the Reverend Doctor Plover as well. Since all the Buntys were coming, and the Misses Hardiment were already engaged elsewhere for that evening, Julia was obliged either to include Eve or be short of one lady, and in the end the balance of her table came first.

Eve always approached these events with mixed feelings. She never had very much money to spare, and what little she did have was always used for things for Luke. Julia had never considered giving her an allowance, but sent discarded clothing in her direction, so she knew that she would be able to take her place at the table without having to blush for her appearance.

Unfortunately, she was not always able to make use of everything that she was given, since Julia's idea of the proper period for mourning a husband was considerably more lax than her own. Even the black gowns that

Julia had thought suitable were of fabrics that Eve considered to be far too rich and gaudy for a widow in her first year of mourning. Out of necessity, Eve had become quite handy with a needle over the years, and she had always made all of Luke's clothes, as well as many of her own. She was therefore able to adapt what her cousin carelessly tossed her way, taking off the trimming and the lace until what remained was much more to her taste. The contrast had pleased Julia; she had never considered that it might please Eve too.

There were aspects of the evening's entertainment to which Eve looked forward with some pleasure. General Sparrow, for instance, was always an interesting conversationalist. He knew about Edmund's distinguished record, and often talked about old army days, making Eve feel as if she had really been able to follow the drum. Lavinia Sparrow, the general's only daughter, was a spinster in her mid forties. Though shy and reserved, she was an amiable person, and enjoyed the same books that absorbed Eve. Sir Laurence and Lady Buckles were always civil, and the vicar's daughter was agreeable enough, although her mother was rather haughty.

Sufficient to outweigh the benefits of any other individuals who might come, however, was the unpleasant person of Horace Bunty. Eve was well aware that this would not be the way in which many ladies would describe him. He was certainly more handsome than his older brother and often appeared superficially to be the more intelligent, since Jeremy was rather slow of speech due to his efforts to overcome a severe stammer. Unfortunately, Horace's good looks were not accompanied by gentlemanly behaviour, and Eve had had to be quite swift in avoiding him on a number of previous occasions. As she got ready, she told herself that she would simply have to take special care if Julia sent her on any errands which took her away from the company.

Needless to say, on the day of the dinner in question, Eve had to delay getting herself ready in order to attend to her cousin's wants. Unfortunately, Julia would never let her forget for very long that she was there on sufferance. She would be sent on little errands and given the tasks that always fell to companions or ladies' maids, whilst Julia continued to comment on how she had taken in her cousin out of charity and how grateful Eve ought to be.

It was a good thing that she had perfected the art of getting ready in a trice, she reflected ironically, as she came away from paying a visit to the nursery to attend to the welfare of her son and baby Thomas. With a party to prepare for, Julia would not go anywhere near the children. Her son would have to do without her presence that day. She never made any kind of enquiry concerning Luke. Like his mother, he needed to be made to understand that he was only there on sufferance.

Even with all the interruptions to her toilette, Eve was the first downstairs, and she took the opportunity to have a brief word with the butler about the evening's arrangements. Greet had always treated her courteously, and it had been thanks to his solid presence on one occasion that she had managed to evade Horace Bunty's advances.

It was as Eve was speaking to Greet that Julia drifted down the stairs. She was in pink silk, trimmed with a large quantity of floss. She was also wearing a diamond set, given to her by her husband on the occasion of their marriage. It included a necklace, bracelets, ear-rings and a tiara, and although Julia had left the tiara upstairs, the whole effect was rather too elaborate for a simple country dinner. It was also very definitely not mourning attire. Had she dressed to impress Horace Bunty in particular, Eve wondered?

17

Reading Eve's expression, Julia said defensively, 'I have gone into half mourning. I thought it was time.'

Eve, who was wearing a modestly cut grey gown with matching lace, said 'In pink?' before she could stop herself.

'It is not pink, it is mauve,' replied Julia with a blithe disregard for the truth. 'In any case, one cannot go on mourning for ever, and I look dreadful without colours.'

General Sparrow and his daughter were the first to be announced. Miss Sparrow, as usual, was dressed in shades of brown, making her look not unlike the bird whose name she shared. Julia mentally compared her toilette with that of her first guest, and her mood, already good, underwent an improvement.

The other guests began to arrive soon afterwards, and Eve had the chance of a few quiet words with Miss Sparrow. 'You will help me if need be, won't you?' she said. 'Horrible Horace is back, and you know what a nuisance he can be.'

'Oh dear me, yes,' Miss Sparrow agreed. 'Be assured that I will do all I can.' Not that she could do a great deal, Eve reflected. On a previous occasion, Julia had sent her to find a handkerchief, and Horace had followed her and trapped her as she was coming out of

18

Mrs Comberton's bedchamber. A tall, strongly built man, he had loured over her, a satisfied smirk spreading across his rather thick lips. Only the advent of Julia's maid had saved her from being seized and kissed. Miss Sparrow could certainly remain close to her in the drawing room, but she could not shadow her on every errand that Julia might devise.

'The delectable Mrs Scorer,' said a smooth voice from behind her, interrupting her musings. With a sinking heart, she turned to see Horace Bunty, faultlessly attired in evening dress.

Eve knew that locally many young ladies found him attractive and, looking at him objectively, which was difficult, she could see why. His figure was good, and showed to admiration in a blue coat, which fitted his shoulders well. He had a fine head of hair, wheat in colour, and cut into a fashionable style. Although the younger of the two brothers, he was his mother's favourite, and received a handsome allowance from his maternal grandmother, who had also made him her heir. For Eve, though, his whole appearance was spoiled by the way in which he carried himself, as if he were quite irresistible to any female with the full possession of her eyesight. She had repulsed him on several occasions, but his lust seemed to be kindled if anything by her lack of interest. Furthermore, there was a shiftiness about his eyes, and a greedy quality to the shape of his mouth that meant that she could never, ever imagine herself trusting him.

None of this showed on her face, however, as she turned, dropped a small curtsy, and replied 'Good evening, Mr Bunty', in an indifferent tone.

'How do you contrive to appear more attractive every time I see you?' he asked, smiling unpleasantly.

'I cannot imagine, sir. Has anyone offered you a glass of sherry?'

Before he could answer, she hurried over to where a footman was standing, and directed him to take a glass to Bunty. That's the first encounter with him over and done, she told herself, before she turned to greet Revd Humphrey Plover and his wife, daughter and brother.

Mr Jeremy Bunty came over to do the same, which did not surprise Eve at all. She had suspected for a long time that the young man was interested in Patience Plover. The vicar's daughter was not plain, despite what Julia had said. Her looks were not spectacular, but her complexion was good, and there was a warmth in her expression which was very engaging. The doting Mrs Bunty would do far better to be throwing a little care and attention in the direction of that deserving but unassuming young couple who, Eve suspected, would be far more likely to be the mainstay of her old age than Horrible Horace.

All those who were invited had accepted the invitation, including Lady Buckles, who was looking thin and tired. Eve made sure that she was found a comfortable seat and, sitting next to her, exchanged thoughts about children and babies. 'Laurence was so upset about the difficult time that I had, that he vows and declares we shall have no more,' Lady Buckles told Eve in an undertone.

'And what do you think?' Eve asked her quietly.

'I am a little apprehensive, but I would like more children,' Lady Buckles admitted. 'The doctor says there is no reason why the next should not be delivered very easily, although he does advise me to wait for a year before even attempting for another baby. Will you come and see my little Dominic soon, Mrs Scorer?'

'As soon as my cousin can spare me,' Eve promised.

Lady Buckles's gentle mouth took on a firm expression. 'I shall insist that she does so. In the meantime, will you take me upstairs later to see Luke?'

'Yes, of course,' Eve answered readily. 'You will be surprised to see how he has grown.'

Soon after this, the bell rang for dinner, and everyone trooped into the dining room, led by Julia, her hand on Sir Laurence's arm. As she might have predicted, Eve brought up the rear and, because he was the youngest gentleman present, Horace was her escort. 'Well this is quite delightful,' Bunty murmured. 'If only I could be certain that you would smile upon me, my pleasure in the evening would be complete.'

'If only I could be certain that you would behave yourself, I would be very willing to smile,' Eve responded calmly.

'But just think what fun I would miss if I always behaved myself,' Horace returned, pinching Eve's thigh under the table as they took their places.

'If you do that again, I will stick a fork in you,' Eve promised. He grinned disbelievingly, but did not attempt that liberty again, so she came to the conclusion that he must have taken her at her word.

Luckily since the party was small, conversation around and across the table was the order of the day, so Eve did not find herself having to converse with the objectionable young man. Instead, she savoured the opportunity of enjoying the variety of dishes on offer. When Julia held a dinner, Eve was frequently excluded from the table, and had to make do with the leftovers.

Some of the conversation concerned Viscount Bradwell, who was due home on leave. 'I do not know why he has to be messing about in boats,' Julia observed, for all the world as if his lordship were entertaining himself with a day's boating on the Thames, rather than being responsible for a ship in His Majesty's Navy.

'Refreshing to discover a young man with a sense of duty,' the general remarked in bluff tones.

'If, indeed, he *is* doing his duty,' Julia replied. 'To my way of thinking, he ought to be here, managing the estate.' Of course, she could afford to make such an assertion, Eve reflected, when there was not the smallest chance of such a thing happening, at least in the immediate future. Shortly after these comments, Julia rose to conduct the ladies to the drawing room.

'This might be a good opportunity for me to see your son,' Lady Buckles suggested, so while the other ladies went to sit down and gossip, Eve conducted her ladyship upstairs to the nursery. A placid and undemanding child, Thomas was asleep already, but Luke was wide awake and was delighted at this extra visit from his Mama, whose gown, he told Lady Buckles, was very pretty.

'Yes, you are right,' Lady Buckles agreed gravely. 'I do declare you have grown at least an inch since last I saw you, Master Scorer.'

'I am wearing breeches now,' Luke told his visitor proudly.

They stayed in the nursery for perhaps ten minutes, but when her ladyship made as if to stand up, she sat down again quickly, saying 'Oh dear, I feel a little giddy. Perhaps I had better wait for a while.'

'Would you like me to fetch Sir Laurence?' Eve asked.

At first Lady Buckles refused vigorously, but after Eve had repeated her suggestion, she agreed that this would be the sensible thing to do. 'If I did not have to negotiate the staircase, I would not trouble him,' she said. 'I have had one or two dizzy spells since my confinement. They are getting less frequent, but they can still take me by surprise.'

'I will fetch him at once,' Eve promised. 'Just don't try to come down on your own.'

'Luke will look after me,' replied Lady Buckles, smiling. Her colour was beginning to come back already.

As Eve hurried down the stairs, she heard a rumble of voices which told her that the gentlemen were leaving the dining room. On her arrival in the hall, it seemed at first as if they must all have gone into the drawing-room already, and she turned right at the bottom of the stairs, to find herself toe to toe with Horace Bunty.

'Well well, how convenient,' he drawled, catching hold of her and pulling her against him.

'Let me go,' she said angrily. She was almost as annoyed with herself for not being cautious as she was with him for lying in wait for her.

'Now you know you don't really mean that,' he answered, tightening his grip.

'I most certainly do,' she replied, renewing her struggles. 'Lady Buckles is feeling faint and I must fetch Sir Laurence at once.'

'One kiss, and I'll let you go,' said Bunty, a smile still pinned to his face. To Eve, his expression looked hot and predatory.

'Certainly not,' she answered. 'How many times do I have to tell you how loathsome I find your advances?'

'Such a pity that Lady Buckles should have to wait,' he murmured, ignoring the last part of her speech.

'Release me, then.'

'I've told you, the solution is in your hands. Kiss me.'

'You're despicable. Let me go at once, or I'll scream.'

'I don't think so,' he retorted, and before she could make any further protest, she was forced back against the staircase and his mouth covered hers, hot, wet, and demanding. She wanted to struggle, but the effect of his tight grip combined with the kiss itself was to deprive her of air, and she began to feel a little light-headed.

Just when she was beginning to think that this appalling experience would go on for ever, the door of the drawing room opened and someone came out. Bunty did release her then, but not before Sir Laurence, for it was he, must have seen her in the younger man's arms.

'Mrs Scorer,' said Sir Laurence with a slight bow. He gave no sign that he had seen anything untoward. 'Might I trouble you to inform me of the whereabouts of my wife?'

Eve was still catching her breath. 'She's upstairs in the nursery, I b'lieve,' Bunty said quickly. 'She felt a little faint.'

Sir Laurence was a kindly, humane man, who liked Mrs Scorer, and did not normally have very much time for Horace Bunty. Anxiety for his wife's present condition clouded his judgement, however, and he said coldly to Eve, 'Better to have fetched me at once, then, rather than waste valuable time dallying in the passage.' Paying the couple no further attention, he hurried up the stairs.

'How dare you?' Eve demanded. She raised her hand to slap his face, but he caught hold of her wrist, making her cry out.

'I only told the truth,' he replied, smirking down at her. That same predatory look was on his face again. 'Very nice,' he said. 'Very nice indeed. I'll have some more of that very soon.'

Eve had not thought that the situation could get any worse. She realized that she was wrong when she heard Julia's voice speaking from the entrance to the drawing room. 'What is the meaning of this?'

'Just a little dalliance,' replied Bunty, releasing Eve, and offering a little bow. 'Excuse me, ladies.'

'That is not the case,' Eve said hotly when he had gone. 'He forced himself upon me, Cousin.'

Julia's face took on a scornful expression. 'Really?' she asked sarcastically. 'A young man of a respectable family, forcing himself upon a penniless widow five years his senior? A likely story. Go to your room. I shall decide what to do with you in the morning.'

Once in her chamber, Eve sat thinking about her likely fate. She did not delude herself. Her value to Julia lay in the fact that she was prepared to make herself useful without remuneration. That, until now, had been sufficient to convince Julia to keep her on. Now, Horace Bunty had returned and everything might change.

Eve knew that Julia was inclined to have a fondness for Mr Bunty. He was just the kind of smooth-talking, rakish man that appealed to her. Unfortunately, however, Mr Bunty had decided to make a play for Eve. Before he had gone to the West Indies for nine months to look to his father's interests there, he had taken the opportunity of making himself objectionable. Eve, widowed only comparatively recently, had at first mistaken his advances for sympathy, and had not repulsed him as firmly as was necessary for a man of his stamp. Luckily, he had departed before his attentions could become noticeable to Julia. Now that he had returned, however, he seemed rather inclined to take up where he had left off; and if this evening was to be an example of his future conduct, then Julia would soon become convinced that he was interested in her impecunious cousin, rather than in herself. After that discovery was made, Eve doubted whether her charity would last for very long.

What would she do if Julia decided to turn her out? Her army pension would be sufficient to keep her and Luke, but she had been counting on saving most of that to go towards her son's education. If she now had to find herself accommodation, and pay for living expenses for the two of them, much of it would be eaten up. It would help if she could find work, but most people who wanted a governess or a companion did not want a small boy as well. Although an appointment teaching in a village school would be ideal, first it would be necessary to find such an appointment.

Not for the first time, Eve felt a spurt of annoyance at Edmund for getting himself killed in action. It was all very well for him to go off and be gallant and heroic. The problem was that his wife was now at the mercy of the kind of rake who could not take no for an answer. No doubt, if Julia did turn her off, Horace would then think that he could pursue her at will. Short of fleeing in the middle of the night in order to evade pursuit, Eve could not think what she might do to stop him.

★ ★ ★

Julia's maid always knew if something had happened to upset her mistress. That evening, after the guests had gone, Mrs Comberton came upstairs in a towering temper. This rather took Fanny by surprise. She had guessed that Mr Bunty was the object of her employer's interest, and was hoping that seeing him again would put her in a good mood. This was clearly not the case.

She had a suspicion why not. She knew what Mr Bunty was like. So did every maid who was unfortunate enough to cross his path. No doubt Mrs Comberton had found him making advances to someone else. Fanny was very glad when at last her mistress dismissed her.

'Go away, wretched girl,' she said impatiently, as soon as she was in her nightgown. 'No, I don't want to go to bed at once. Do I look as though I would be able to sleep? Hand me my dressing gown, and don't be all night about it either. Now get out of my sight. I want to write a letter.'

After the maid had gone, she sat down at her dressing-table, took out pen, paper and ink, and sat down to finish a letter to her brother-in-law. It was a letter that she had begun several days before. Now, she finished it with a heartfelt, if not strictly accurate complaint about Eve. That done, she retired at last to bed and slept the deep, untroubled sleep only enjoyed either by those with clear consciences, or by those with no conscience at all.

3

Whatever Julia's intentions might be with regard to her future, Eve did not make the mistake of thinking that her cousin would be up betimes to deal with the matter. She, however, rose at her usual hour, attending to all her customary duties. Whatever Julia might find to throw at her head, it would not be that she had become idle!

After having breakfast in the nursery, she went downstairs, intending to go for her daily interview with the cook. She was on her way to the kitchen when the front-door bell rang. Hearing men's voices, she hurried on her way, not wanting to be found by Mr Bunty, if indeed it was he who had come at such a time. So early a call on his part would be entirely unprecedented, but Eve had no way of knowing what conversations might have taken place after she had gone to her room. Might Mr Bunty believe that her reputation was now so blackened that she would welcome almost any kind of escape, even down to becoming his mistress? She shuddered at the thought.

She had barely had time to greet the cook,

when one of the footmen came into the kitchen with a message that a gentleman had asked for Mrs Scorer and was waiting in the book-room.

'It's not Mr Bunty, is it?' Eve asked suspiciously.

'No, ma'am,' the footman replied reassuringly. Engaged to one of the chambermaids, he had often been tempted to flatten Mr Bunty for his amorous attentions to his beloved. 'It's a gentleman from London — here on business, he said.'

'Business? With me?'

'That's what he said, ma'am.'

'Oh. Thank you, Robert.'

Eve walked slowly to the book-room, wondering what on earth this could be about. The only other time she had received a visit from London since Edmund's death had been to do with her pension from the army. Heaven forbid they should have decided to cease paying it, for then she would be destitute indeed.

She arrived at the entrance to the book-room at the same time as Greet, the butler, appeared with a tray on which stood a decanter and glasses.

'I made so bold as to offer the gentleman wine, ma'am,' said the butler.

'It is what Mrs Comberton would want,

I'm sure,' Eve replied, as she entered the room.

Her visitor was a man only a little taller than herself, and he looked to be in his early fifties. His attire indicated that he was a professional man. He bowed politely, and came forward saying, 'Forgive me, madam, for this unexpected visit, but I have important news to communicate to you which could not easily be conveyed by post. My name is Trafford, and I am a partner of Sykes, Morgan and Trafford, a company of solicitors that is fixed in the City of London.'

'I am Eve Scorer,' Eve replied, curtsying. 'How may I help you, sir?' She poured Mr Trafford a glass of wine from the decanter that Greet had left.

'I believe that the boot is rather on the other foot,' Mr Trafford replied, permitting a small smile to cross his rather thin features. 'I have some news to impart which is very much to your advantage.'

'My advantage?' Eve echoed, much puzzled. 'They are not increasing my widow's pension, are they?'

'I beg your pardon?' asked the lawyer.

'Is this matter nothing to do with the army, then?'

'I know nothing at all about your pension,' Mr Trafford told her. 'May we be seated, then

I will be able to open the whole matter for you?'

Eve begged his pardon, and after they had sat down, Trafford in a chair at a table in the window, and Eve opposite him, the lawyer took some papers out of a leather case which he had set down on the table beforehand.

'Before I can disclose the matter which benefits you, I fear that I must give you some sad tidings,' he said solemnly. 'I have to inform you of the death of Mme Lascelles.'

There was an awkward silence. 'I fear you have the advantage of me,' Eve said eventually. 'Naturally, it is grievous to hear of the death of any person, but I fear that this name is quite unknown to me. Are you sure that you have come to the right house? Or does your news concern some other person living here, perhaps?'

'You might be wiser if I were to tell you that before her marriage, she was a Miss Cramer,' the lawyer suggested a little diffidently.

'I might be — but I fear I am not,' Eve responded with a wry smile. 'Although the name is not entirely unfamiliar. What was her Christian name, if you please?'

Mr Trafford shuffled his papers around. 'Her Christian name, Mrs Scorer, was Rosemary, and she was your mother's aunt.'

'Her aunt?' repeated Eve. 'But I thought that my mother's aunt was called Vera.'

'That would have been your grandfather's sister,' replied Mr Trafford. 'I am speaking now of your grandmother's sister.'

Eve looked at him in astonishment. 'But I thought that my grandmother was an only child.'

'She might as well have been,' answered the lawyer. 'This lady was not your grandmother's full sister. Your great-grandparents married when Rosemary was only ten. Very soon afterwards, she went to live in France with her paternal relations, possibly because the new family arrangements did not work out as well as hoped.'

'You say that she was married. Does her husband survive her?'

Trafford shook his head. 'She had no living relatives apart from yourself,' he told her. 'She died two weeks ago. Unfortunately, due to the death of one of my clerks at about the same time, her papers were in some disorder and it was not possible to discover the names of any relatives before she was laid to rest. But as soon as I did so, I made haste to come here.'

'That is very good of you,' replied Eve. 'I shall make sure that her name is mentioned in prayers at the parish church. I trust that she did not have to suffer the indignity of a pauper's grave?'

'No indeed. The reason for my visit is not essentially a pastoral one, but a practical one. Do you not remember that I said I had something to disclose that would be to your advantage?'

'Has she mentioned me in her will?' Eve asked tentatively.

'She has indeed,' Mr Trafford answered, shuffling his papers again. 'It is quite simple. There is only one bequest. Madame Lascelles has left you everything that she possessed.'

'Everything?' Eve echoed, her voice coming out much squeakier than she had intended. 'To me?'

'She certainly appears to have done so,' Mr Trafford said. 'She is quite specific. 'To my great-niece Mrs Edmund Scorer, formerly Miss Eve Colby'.'

'What does she leave me, if you please?' asked Eve, telling herself that she would be very happy with twenty pounds. It would, after all, be equivalent to the year's salary that she might be getting if she were not fetching and carrying for her cousin for nothing.

'Ah yes,' answered Mr Trafford. 'To my great-niece . . . ' He paused and looked down at his papers. The pause seemed to Eve to last for hours. 'The sum of ten thousand pounds — '

'Ten thousand!' exclaimed Eve.

'Ten thousand pounds,' repeated Trafford, 'conditional upon her also accepting my bookshop and library on Clerkenwell Green, and upon her living there for six months, after which she will be free to dispose of the said shop and retain the proceeds.'

'Six months? A bookshop?' Eve had always prided herself on being level-headed. She now found herself feeling like one of those foolish persons who cannot seem to take information in properly.

'It seems a very strange way to leave a property, certainly,' said Trafford. 'I fear there is no way of getting round this condition. It is very carefully set out.'

'What will happen to the bequest should I refuse to go to Clerkenwell?'

Mr Trafford looked down at the paper in his hand. 'The money, together with the proceeds from the shop, would go to a Mr Belmont of Half Moon Street.'

'I suppose he must also be a relative,' Eve speculated.

'Not as far as I can tell,' the lawyer responded. 'I made discreet enquiries about him, not knowing what your feelings about the bequest might be, and have been unable

38

to locate him so far. He is not to receive anything should you accept the bequest. However, the will does stipulate that should you accept the bequest and then decide to sell the shop later, then Mr Belmont must be given the first opportunity of purchasing it.'

'What is the shop like?' Eve asked the lawyer. 'Have you seen it, sir?'

'I have.'

'Is it presently open for business?'

'It was being run as a business right until the tragic death of my late client. Since then, the shop and library have been locked up and I hold the key.'

'Was her death unexpected?' Eve asked curiously. 'I thought that she was an old lady.'

'I regret to have to inform you . . . ' The lawyer paused, glancing first at Eve, then away again.

'You need not be afraid of telling me about what happened to her,' Eve said calmly. 'Over the past five years, I have lost my husband, my father, and both my husband's parents, three of them while I was at the bedside.'

'She fell down the stairs at the property, and died there,' Trafford said bluntly.

'Perhaps she became faint as she was coming down.'

'Perhaps,' agreed the lawyer, 'although she was very sprightly for her age. Do you now understand the conditions of your inheritance?'

'I believe so,' she answered cautiously. 'I must reside in Clerkenwell and open the shop for six months, or I forfeit everything. Is that correct?'

'Quite correct,' Trafford agreed.

'Once I have fulfilled those conditions, however, I may sell the bookshop and keep the proceeds, but I must offer it to Mr Belmont first.'

'I couldn't have put it better myself,' declared Trafford, getting to his feet. 'I would strongly advise you to accept the bequest, but I will not press you for an answer immediately. I am staying at the hostelry in the village. You may communicate your decision to me there.'

At this point, the door opened, and Julia drifted in, wreathed in smiles because there was a man for her to charm. 'Eve, my love, will you not introduce me to your guest?'

Eve was not deceived. Once Mr Trafford had gone, she would be lambasted for receiving a man — no, for presuming that she was in a position to receive *any* guests in this house where she was little more than a servant. She did what Julia asked, however, introducing her to Mr Trafford who, unsurprisingly, smirked rather fatuously. It was, Eve had noticed, a common reaction to Julia's beauty among most men, particularly those who did not know her well.

'And what brings you to this part of the country?' Julia asked him.

'I am here on a matter of business which concerns Mrs Scorer,' he replied. Charmed with Mrs Comberton's beauty he might be; he was still too professional a man to discuss someone's private affairs with another.

'With Eve?' exclaimed Julia, almost as if he had suggested that his business had been with the mantelpiece or the carpet. 'Good heavens!'

Trafford's expression changed subtly. 'Yes, with Mrs Scorer,' he replied frostily. 'I must be going.'

'Will you not remain and take some luncheon with us?' asked Julia, smiling. 'Then you can tell us more about your . . . business.'

'Thank you, no,' replied Trafford. 'I have promised myself a day or two's walking in the hills, and as today is fine, I will not miss the opportunity.'

'For how long will you be remaining in the vicinity?' Eve asked him, as they shook hands.

'Until the end of the week, by which time, I must have your decision. Good morning to you.'

After Greet had shown Mr Trafford out,

Julia turned to Eve. Every vestige of amiability was gone from her face, and when she spoke, her tone was hard and brittle. 'Shameless! To entertain a man alone like that! But then, after last night's behaviour. I wonder that I am surprised.'

Eve looked at her in astonishment. She had honestly forgotten last night's events, at least for the time being, in the excitement of the morning's disclosures. 'I beg your pardon?'

'And so you might well,' Julia answered. 'What must the servants think of your behaviour, you . . . you hussy?'

'I'm not a hussy,' Eve replied with dignity, 'and I am sure that the servants have too much sense to suppose it.'

Julia flushed with mortification at the implication of her cousin's remark. 'Oh really? I suppose I imagined that you had been devouring Horace Bunty at the bottom of the stairs last night.'

'I was not devouring him,' Eve declared vehemently. 'The very idea makes me feel sick.'

'Very likely,' answered Julia with heavy sarcasm. 'That is not the tale that Mr Bunty tells. Who is more likely to be telling the truth, do you think? An eligible young man with his pick of the neighbourhood, or a penniless widow at her last prayers?'

'I would have thought that *you* would be more likely to believe the cousin who has lived with you for over a year, and who has never given you cause to doubt her veracity,' said Eve, looking at Julia steadily.

The other woman looked away. 'Of course you have your own version of events,' she said dismissively. 'What was that lawyer here for, anyway?'

'He has come to inform me of a bequest,' Eve answered, trying not to sound triumphant. 'I have inherited some money and a bookshop.'

'Indeed?' responded Julia, looking as if she might enquire as to whether Eve had managed this through a careful plan of seduction. 'In that case — '

Eve interrupted her quickly. She did not know whether Julia intended to turn her out or not, but she had no intention of allowing her that satisfaction. 'In that case, I shall, of course, be leaving you very soon,' she said. 'I am grateful for your hospitality extended to me in time of need, but thanks to this bequest I shall now be in the fortunate position of being able to provide for Luke and myself.'

'I do not know whether it is very convenient to let you go just now,' Julia replied petulantly. 'There is Thomas to be thought of.'

'Thomas only needs his nurse,' replied Eve. 'I am sure you will manage very well without me.'

'Much you care,' Julia answered. 'It will be a novel situation for you, having to look out for fortune hunters.' She did not need to say that in her opinion the fortune would be the only thing that would make the taking on of Eve and Luke remotely palatable: it was written all over her face.

4

The ship's surgeon continued his examination, whilst his patient lay with gritted teeth. 'Nothing's broken, sir,' he said eventually. 'But you fell very awkwardly.'

'What on earth does the navy pay you to come up with that brilliant diagnosis?' asked the other man ironically.

'Get that down you, Ballantyne, and stop being so damned rude,' said a third man, crossing the cabin with two glasses, one of which he gave to the doctor and the other to his patient.

'To continue,' went on the doctor, taking the drink offered to him, 'your thigh is very badly bruised and you've twisted your knee. The damage isn't permanent, but you'll be in pain for a time. You ought to keep off that leg as much as possible.'

'Blast! The first time home in two years and I have to go hobbling around on a stick!'

'That'll teach you to go down amongst the horses during a storm,' observed the third man impassively.

'What else was I to do?' demanded the patient from his position on the leather couch. 'One of your crew told me that a horse had broken free. I couldn't risk it falling and hurting itself and others as well.'

'Whereas it fell and hurt you instead.'

'Yes, but at least I managed to get it tethered up again.'

The doctor finished his rum. 'Well, gentlemen, I'll leave you now. I'll come and look at that leg again tomorrow.'

'Another?' the captain asked his guest, holding up the bottle.

Ballantyne nodded. 'There really is no need for you to give up your cabin,' he said. 'I'll be quite all right with my officers.'

'Not if you're to rest that leg,' the captain replied. 'So *I'll* go in with *my* officers. Would you like me to help you to bed before I go?'

'Thank you, no. If you would be so good as to send for Correy, my batman, he'll look after me.'

'It shall be done.'

'This is very good of you, Bradwell,' said Ballantyne before the other man left.

'Nonsense, m'dear fellow,' answered Bradwell, his hand on the door handle. 'I depend upon you to give me a game or two of piquet by way of entertainment whilst you're here.'

★ ★ ★

It did not take the two men very long to strike up a friendship on the voyage back from Egypt. Just as Viscount Bradwell had chosen a career at sea, so Jason Ballantyne had made a positive decision to join the army, and both men had risen in the ranks as much by merit as by purchase.

'M'father would be very glad if I were to leave the navy,' Bradwell confided one evening after they had retired to Ballantyne's temporary quarters after dinner. 'Every time I think I might oblige him, we get another piece of action, which convinces me that I'd be missing too much.'

Ballantyne gave a bark of laughter. 'My mother makes very much the same kind of noises,' he said. 'I see no reason to fall in with her wishes at the moment. Her jointure is secure and very adequate for her needs, none of my property is entailed, and I've an excellent steward. Unlike you, my dear fellow, I don't need to worry about handing on a title.'

'Carry on getting yourself mentioned in despatches and that situation will soon be altered,' Bradwell retorted, pouring them both a glass of brandy. 'Anyway, I have an heir already. My father is in excellent health, and my brother, God rest his soul, fathered a son before his demise last year. The lad is making good progress, apparently.'

Ballantyne admired the colour of the brandy before taking a sip. 'Your father keeps you well informed, I gather.'

Bradwell laughed. 'Not he! He's only capable of writing every six months telling me what the cattle raised at market, or how much wheat was taken off the largest of my fields. What the deuce am I supposed to know or care about such matters?'

'Presumably the income from your lands is responsible in part for sustaining your captaincy,' Ballantyne pointed out mildly.

'True enough. I stand corrected,' the viscount agreed, raising his glass. 'God bless Father and his acres. It all means nothing to me, but I thank God that it's to his taste, and that he's able and willing to get on with it. I'd be obliged to see to it myself, otherwise, and a deucedly poor fist I'd make of it.'

Ballantyne raised his glass as well. 'God bless all those who plant and reap for the country's needs. Who does keep you informed, then?'

'My sister-in-law keeps me abreast of all the family gossip. I hardly need to go home at all in order to find anything out. Anyone would think that she didn't want me to settle down and have a family of my own!'

'Don't you?' asked the colonel, noting his

companion's ironic tone.

'You know, part of me would like it,' replied Bradwell thoughtfully. 'It ain't that I don't like the ladies, God bless'em. It's just that I find it hard to think of one that I'd prefer over this one.' He patted the panelling of his ship. 'Don't tell my sister-in-law, though. I like to keep her guessing.'

'I hope she writes a better hand than my mother,' Ballantyne remarked. 'Sometimes I can barely make out a word she's written. The last letter but one, I thought that she was telling me that her white horse had become caught in a mangle. When I looked more closely, I realized that she was informing me that the whole house had contracted measles.'

Bradwell laughed, and poured them more brandy. 'My sister-in-law writes quite a fair hand, but why the deuce she thinks I want to hear about some of this stuff I shall never know. Look at the length of this most recent offering!' He held up several sheets for the colonel's inspection. 'Five pages! And signed 'your affectionate sister, Julia Comberton'. Well, I could do with a little less verbiage, but at least she does write.'

'Comberton, did you say?'

'It's the family name, old boy.'

'I'd forgotten. Is your estate situated near Sheffield?'

'That's right. What of it?'

'By the most astonishing coincidence, I find myself obliged to call upon your sister-in-law.'

'Indeed?'

'Well, not your sister-in-law strictly speaking. Her companion, a Mrs Scorer, is the widow of one of my officers, and this will be the first chance that I will have had to call upon her in order to return her husband's effects.'

'Really? Then you might as well travel with me. I'm planning to make my way there as soon as we've docked. Have you made any travel arrangements?'

Ballantyne shook his head. 'Not as yet.'

'Then bear me company. It's a tedious stretch on your own.' There was a short silence. Then Bradwell asked, 'Have you met the lady?'

'Mrs Scorer? I've not had the pleasure,' the colonel answered.

'That's an interesting turn of phrase,' Bradwell murmured.

'What do you mean?' the colonel asked, wrinkling his brow.

'From what Julia tells me in this letter, she's in the process of pursuing a male guest in the most blatant way possible,' Bradwell replied. 'M'sister-in-law is very torn between her duty to provide a home for her cousin and her need to protect the morals of her household.'

Ballantyne frowned. 'I didn't get that impression of Mrs Scorer from her husband's description,' he remarked.

Bradwell gave a snort of laughter. 'How many men carry a rose-tinted picture of their sweetheart or wife, only to find out that she's played them false? I could think of a dozen.'

The colonel's complexion darkened. 'Yes, so could I,' he agreed.

'Had your fingers burned, too?' asked the viscount acutely.

'Simply angry that a gallant officer might have had his name besmirched by the actions of his widow,' the colonel answered shortly.

'Just so,' agreed Bradwell, getting out the cards. 'It's exactly why I prefer to be wedded to the *Dauntless*. Piquet?'

★ ★ ★

Later that evening, after Viscount Bradwell had left Ballantyne to settle down, the colonel got out Captain Scorer's few belongings. They included his sword and medals, his watch and snuffbox, his signet ring and his prayer book, signed by his father and given to him when he was ten years old: a tiny collection, really, to stand for a man's life.

There was another item belonging to the captain which was not with the other things, and this was a miniature of his wife. The captain had shown it to the colonel when he lay dying, and had spoken eloquently about his wife's courage, her loyalty, her kindness to his parents, her fine qualities as a mother.

'Look after them, sir,' he had said on that last evening, when Ballantyne had gone to sit by his bed. His voice had been so weak that the colonel had barely been able to hear him, and he had had to lean very close to him to catch his words. 'Promise me . . .'

'On my honour,' the colonel had replied. Then Scorer had begun to choke, Ballantyne had lifted him gently to help him breathe, and like a child knowing that he had reached a place of safety, the captain had turned his head towards Jason's neck, and died in his commanding officer's arms.

After that, Ballantyne had seen to the burial with as much honour as was possible in the field and had packed up Scorer's belongings with care; but for some reason, he had kept the miniature amongst his own effects. If asked, he might have said that having promised to care for his officer's widow, it somehow seemed wrong just to pack her picture away in the dark without reminding himself of the one whom he had engaged himself to guard and protect. If he were honest with himself, however, he knew in his heart of hearts that he had another reason.

Perhaps it was because Captain Scorer had spoken about his wife with so much feeling, but as Ballantyne had looked at the picture, it had seemed to him that the qualities which the captain had mentioned seemed to shine out of her face, until by the time the colonel had boarded the *Dauntless*, he was in the habit of taking the picture out and looking at it every day, as if it were some kind of talisman.

He told himself that he was not really being foolishly sentimental. He did not even know the lady. He was not in any danger of imagining that some relationship already existed between them, or was likely to blossom in the future. Nevertheless, it occurred to him that she sounded like the ideal soldier's wife. It would please him very much to meet her; then, perhaps, to meet her again.

Now, however, his conversation with Bradwell had left him a prey to doubts.

He had turned aside the viscount's question about his own experience. The fact of the matter was that he had not been very lucky in love. A tall, broadly built man, with a fine head of jet-black hair and striking, if not handsome, features, he had physically matured early. Consequently, he had found himself the target of predatory females since he reached the age of seventeen, when a friend of his mother had seduced him. He had never told his mother, and her friend had died several years before; but his boyish pride had been hurt by the encounter, for the lady had pretended affection for him, and had then laughed at him when he was in the throes of his infatuation for her.

Some years after this encounter, as a very junior army officer, he had been sent to the home of his colonel to take his wife a message. This officer had been full of praises for his wife's excellent qualities, but after she had offered Ballantyne a drink, and then sent him glances that were quite unmistakable in their intention, he had left in disgust, having delivered the message as quickly as possible. After much heart-searching he had decided not to tell his superior about his wife's perfidy, and when the man died in action shortly afterwards he was glad he had not done so.

The years had taught him to be wary of women, and although he enjoyed casual relationships with obliging females, he had fought shy of anything more permanent. There had been something about Mrs Scorer that had tempted him to think again. Now, he found himself uncertain. On the one hand, he had respected Captain Scorer's judgement; on the other, his wife must have been very lonely at times with her husband far across the sea, and after his death, grief could have caused her to act foolishly. If such was the case, then it behoved Edmund's commanding officer to remind her of what was due to her husband's memory.

After a moment's hesitation, he put her miniature back amongst his own belongings. She might or might not be as virtuous as her husband had maintained; for his part, he would try to reserve judgement.

* * *

In the event, the two men's tentative plans to travel together came to nothing after all. No sooner had the ship docked at Portsmouth, than a messenger came aboard with a letter for Colonel Ballantyne. He read it swiftly, then went to find Bradwell, who had been up on deck overseeing their arrival.

'It appears that our ways are to part after all,' he said. 'I am summoned elsewhere.'

'I shall miss your company,' the viscount replied. A man with some years' experience as a serving officer, he knew better than to ask what matter needed to be attended to. 'But, of course, you will be visiting us when your business is done, in order to do your duty by Mrs Scorer. Unless you would like to commission me to take the sword to her when I go?'

Ballantyne shook his head. 'No,' he replied. 'I owe it to Edmund Scorer to see his widow in person. It is a matter of duty.'

5

'This is most inconvenient,' Julia complained, not for the first time. 'I am not sure that I should not expect you to give me some notice.' It had not taken Eve very long to decide to accept her kinswoman's bequest. For two pins, she could almost have run after Mr Trafford as he left the house to tell him of her decision, and she had written to him as soon as she had a moment to herself after his departure. Once her letter was written, she had gone to find Julia to inform her that she would be travelling with the lawyer when he returned to London.

'Only servants are expected to give notice, surely,' Eve replied calmly.

Julia had the grace to blush. 'You know that that is not what I meant,' she muttered, without meeting her cousin's eye. 'It is simply that I cannot possibly spare a maid to travel with you at this time.'

'I had never supposed that you would,' Eve responded.

As it turned out, Eve had a more than adequate escort to accompany her on her journey to London. Miss Sparrow had a sister two years older than herself who was married and living in London, and to whom she paid a visit every year with very little pleasure. She was delighted to travel with Mrs Scorer and Mr Trafford, and she also offered to stay with Eve for the time being, thus solving another problem. Eve might consider that she would be able to live in the country in a cottage with just her son for company; she knew very well, however, that for the sake of propriety, she would need a chaperon in Town, and had been wondering how best to obtain one, without advertising or going to an agency.

'I do not want to deprive your sister of your company,' Eve ventured.

'Well I do,' answered Miss Sparrow frankly. 'My sister is for ever pointing out how foolish I was to stay at home and nurse my mother instead of finding a husband for myself. I shall be glad of the excuse to stay elsewhere and to simply visit my sister from time to time. I am sure that you will soon find someone agreeable to reside with you once you are fixed in Town.'

Eve very much enjoyed travelling to London, for she had seldom visited the capital city. For Luke, the whole journey was a novelty, and he spent all his time looking out of the windows and asking questions of whoever happened to be feeling sufficiently wide awake at the time. He was inclined to miss Thomas at first, but Miss Sparrow, who seemed to have a natural affinity with children, despite her childless state, soon engaged him in conversation. In no time they were competing over who might be the first to see a brown dog, or a cow with horns.

They stopped more frequently than Eve suspected Mr Trafford would have done had he been travelling alone, but the needs of such a mixed party had to be considered. To his credit, he made no complaint about the time the journey took, and spent a good deal of it in reading. Eve would have liked to ask him the name of his book, and enquire whether he had ever patronized her newly inherited establishment in Clerkenwell. She said nothing because she did not want to look as if she was advertising for business.

It had been decided that they would put up at the Angel, Islington that night. Once they had reached the inn, Mr Trafford bade them farewell, telling them that he would meet them the following morning outside the bookshop in Clerkenwell Green.

'I was going to say 'outside Mme Lascelles's bookshop'. Of course it is yours now,' said Mr Trafford, bowing apologetically to Eve.

'You're a woman of property now, my

dear,' said Miss Sparrow.

The next day, Eve hired a carriage from The Angel to take her to Clerkenwell Green. No doubt she would eventually get used to being able to do such things, she reflected. For now, such novelty was an agreeable luxury to be savoured. She went alone, since Miss Sparrow had kindly offered to stay behind and look after Luke while she visited the shop. This kind of outing was hardly likely to appeal to a boy of six.

On her arrival, she got out of the carriage and stood looking about her. Her first impression of her inheritance from the outside was that it seemed a very respectable place. The sign above the shop door proclaimed 'Bookshop and Circulating Library' with the words 'Proprietress R. Cramer' underneath. Clearly Mme Lascelles had reverted to her maiden name, perhaps because of the war with France.

Given its name, Clerkenwell Green appeared to be a rather grey place. She thought of the village green at home, grasscovered, with a pond set to one side, on which ducks and other birds were to be found. Here, there was not so much as a tree or a blade of grass to be seen. Yet it was a pleasant prospect.

Across the green in front of her stood a turnstile leading into another road or close, with a handsome-looking church facing her way. To her left and slightly downhill stood a fine public building, probably less than fifty years old. To her right lay the road by which she had come after leaving the Angel and travelling down St John Street.

At that point a hackney approached and Mr Trafford jumped down, flushed with mortification and stammering apologies for his lateness.

'Not at all,' replied Eve. 'It is only just the hour.' As if to confirm her words, a church clock chimed eleven.

'You are very good, ma'am, very good,' said Trafford, much flustered. 'But I should have been here early to receive you. Well, let us go in and I will show you round.' He took out a key. 'There are two doors into the property as you can see. This key opens the front door which leads into the private part of the house.'

'Is there no one on the premises?' asked Eve, pausing only to give instructions to the carriage driver to wait until she was ready. 'Were no servants retained to care for the property?'

Trafford pursed his lips. 'There's a couple who worked for your kinswoman who are hoping to keep their places,' he told her. 'They are acting as caretakers for the present. I don't know how useful they will be. They have been told to keep out of the way this morning.'

Eve said nothing, but reflected that they must surely be more useful than nobody at all.

The front door opened into a hall, with stairs leading up to a landing straight ahead. On the right-hand side was a door, which Mr Trafford unlocked for her. 'As you see, you can keep this door locked, and thus maintain your family's privacy.' The door led into a spacious room, lined with bookshelves, on which books were arranged in what appeared to be a systematic fashion. They did not seem to be new, so Eve was not surprised when Mr Trafford said, 'This is the library.' She wandered over to the shelves and was pleased to find some of her favourites there.

'The bookshop is behind,' Mr Trafford told her, and he invited her to enter another room, smaller than the first, and also lined with shelves. There was a number of unopened boxes stacked in the middle of the room. 'I suspect that this is new stock, which Mme Lascelles did not have time to open before she died,' he went on.

'Where is the living area?' Eve asked him.

'This way,' he replied. He led her back into the hall, and up the stairs which, although not poky, were not exactly spacious either. Once in the living quarters, however, Eve was pleasantly surprised. A fine drawing room, which lay above the library, was decorated in pale blue, and the furnishings, in blue and gold, were well chosen and looked quite new.

'St Paul's is in that direction,' Trafford told her, pointing to the left, 'but not quite visible from here, I'm afraid. You have a fine view of St James's, Clerkenwell.'

The rest of the accommodation, dining-room, study and four bedrooms, with attic rooms as well, was just as pleasing.

'What of the kitchen?' Eve asked curiously.

'That is at the back of the hall downstairs,' replied Mr Trafford. 'I did not think you would want to see it.'

'I want to see everything.'

'I suspect that the Todds are in there,' he told her, as they descended the stairs. 'They are the couple that I told you about. There is a room directly behind it where they live.'

They entered the kitchen to find a thin, depressed-looking female standing at the kitchen table stirring something in a bowl, whilst a swarthy man with long brown straggly hair sat watching her. At their appearance he got to his feet. He was quite tall and thin, with a slight stoop. He looked to be much older than the woman, but that might have been because of his stance.

'Ah, Todd,' said Mr Trafford. 'Mrs Scorer, this is Tim Todd and his wife, Biddy. This is Mrs Scorer, who is to be mistress here. If you wish to retain your places, she is the one you need to speak to politely.'

'Pleased to meet you, ma'am, I'm sure,' said Biddy Todd, curtsying, her eyes lowered. 'We'd like the chance to give satisfaction, wouldn't we, Tim?'

'Aye,' the man mumbled, bowing, then adding 'ma'am' rather belatedly.

'Let us see if we suit one another,' said Eve with a smile. 'What are your duties?'

'I do general work, ma'am,' said Biddy. 'Tim sees to the stove and sweeps the yard. He was shot by a Frenchman and he can't think quite straight now.'

'Very well,' said Eve. 'We'll talk more later.' She felt a little embarrassed because neither of the Todds returned her smile.

'I'm not sure how useful Todd will be,' said Mr Trafford, echoing his earlier words as he handed her into the carriage, their inspection completed. 'It might be wise to let him go.'

'He is an old soldier,' Eve said simply. 'Remember that my husband died in the service of his country.'

'Of course, I understand your position,' Trafford replied hastily. 'But you will need

64

more than the Todds to look after you and to help with the shop.'

'I'll think about that tomorrow. In the meantime, I am anxious to get back to my son.'

6

It was almost dark when the private closed carriage and pair carrying Colonel Ballantyne clattered into the main entrance of Walmer Castle. Those wanting to find any identifying features on this equipage would have been disappointed, for it was quite undistinguished, as were the horses that pulled it.

It drew up inside the courtyard, and the groom seated next to the coachman sprang down to help its occupant to get out. The colonel gritted his teeth. The assistance was necessary, but he hated to be so dependent upon another, and he uttered his words of thanks in the stilted manner of one who would much rather have said 'be damned to you'.

For a moment or two he lingered, looking about him at the surroundings, barely visible now in the gathering gloom. There were a few distant lights, which might be those of a village, and others in the opposite direction which almost certainly indicated the presence of a vessel out at sea. Looking up, he saw that there were candles burning in the castle itself.

He had not visited this place before, and

glanced round again, before limping towards what appeared to be the front door. The groom hurried to help him, and was waved away with an impatient gesture. 'Have done, man, have done. I'll do now.'

The noise of the carriage had alerted the occupants of the castle to the visitor's arrival, and the door was opened by a servant in livery as Ballantyne was just setting his foot on the bottom step. The footman was tall, nearly six feet in height. As the newcomer ascended, it became clear that he was going to top him by quite a few inches.

'Colonel Ballantyne to see Mr Pitt,' said that gentleman.

'Ah yes, you are expected, Colonel,' answered the footman, somewhat relieved. 'May I take your things?'

Ballantyne handed his greatcoat and his hat to the footman, revealing the red coat with blue facings and gold lace of an officer of Dragoons.

The footman looked up at the colonel's face and felt glad that this was not an unwelcome visitor. Even given the gentleman's obvious infirmity, he would be a trifle difficult to eject. It was not simply the man's height and breadth of shoulder, or the sword at his side, which looked serviceable rather than ornamental, as did the boots on his feet;

rather, it was the implacable nature of his expression, and his stance, both of which seemed to indicate that he would not easily be swayed from a course of action that he had once decided upon.

His face was interesting. His dark wavy hair was swept back from his brow, and fell naturally into curls which other, more fashion-conscious men would have slept for hours in curling rags to achieve. His nose was a pronounced aquiline, and his chin jutted out firmly, with the potential to become arrogantly aggressive should the need arise. His mouth was rather thin-lipped but well-shaped, and his grey eyes looked full of intelligence. All of his skin currently exposed to view had a tanned appearance, as if he had served in sunny climes, and frequently out of doors.

'Please follow me, sir,' said the footman.

Ballantyne picked up a bottle that he had brought in with him from the carriage and which he had set down on a small table whilst he shed his outer garments. 'For Mr Pitt's birthday,' he remarked.

'I'm sure he will be delighted, sir,' said the footman.

Pitt was sitting alone in the drawing room, and he rose to greet his guest. 'It's good to see you, Ballantyne,' he said calmly. 'Have you dined?'

Ballantyne shook his head. 'I decided to press on here,' he answered, shaking the hand that Pitt held out. 'I was sure you'd have something special to offer me on your birthday.'

Pitt smiled thinly. He was a tall man, although not as tall as his visitor, and rather lean, with a prominent nose. 'If you wanted something special on my birthday, you should have gone to my party,' he replied, indicating a chair for his visitor then sitting down himself.

'Yes, I understand they're holding one for you in London tonight,' the colonel answered, unbuckling his sword and laying it down, then easing himself carefully into the chair that his host had indicated. 'Canning has written a song especially for the occasion.'

'I don't know why they bother,' replied Pitt, steepling his fingers together. 'They know I take no pleasure in such occasions.'

'Well I'm sure their pleasure will be more than adequate to cover the loss of your presence. I've brought you a gift, by the way.'

'If it's money you can take it back,' Pitt answered shortly. Ballantyne smiled. Pitt's desperate financial situation was well known, but he had refused gifts of money from London merchants and even from the King, preferring to sell his own house at Holwood, and to accept a loan to cover the rest of the debt.

'It's not money,' answered Ballantyne, producing the bottle. 'It's port; but I will take it back, if you like. After all, it's probably barely drinkable after being shaken up in my groom's saddlebag all the way from London.'

A spot of colour appeared on each of Pitt's cheekbones. 'Shaken up! My God, it'll never recover. That's no way to treat port, Ballantyne!'

The colonel threw back his head and roared with laughter. Those who considered him an austere, humourless man — and there were quite a lot of them — would have revised their opinion on hearing that full, rich sound. 'There's a case for you at the nearest hostelry,' he said reassuringly. 'It travelled by my order, and very slowly. The bottle I have with me came in my carriage. I thought we might share it tonight.'

'Share?' echoed Pitt, a flicker of humour at the back of his eyes. 'Don't you remember that I was prescribed a bottle of port a day from the age of fourteen?'

'Certainly I do,' replied the colonel promptly, 'and if you've had none of your allocated dose today, I should be very much surprised.'

The look of amusement on Pitt's face increased. The man sitting with him was one of the few whose company he was prepared to tolerate. 'You're right, of course,' he replied. 'Very well, I'll share.'

'Will you also share the reason for which you sent for me?' Ballantyne asked.

'Later,' answered Pitt, getting up to ring the bell. 'Griffiths will take you to your room and we'll talk over dinner.'

Up in the cosy bedroom that had been prepared for him, Jason Ballantyne stripped to the waist and washed and shaved, whilst his host's valet unpacked a clean shirt and coat for the evening. The colonel refused help with shaving. He had looked after himself on too many occasions to want to be molly-coddled now.

Why had Pitt sent for him, he wondered, sitting down and rubbing his left leg to try to ease the ache in it. It had to be for something unofficial. Pitt himself had resigned from the office of prime minister the previous year over the issue of Catholic emancipation in Ireland. Since his resignation, he had spent more time here at Walmer than in Parliament, and Addington now occupied the highest office in the land.

Pitt had successfully steered the country through nine years of war, and everyone in the country had greeted the Peace of Amiens with a sigh of relief. Yet Ballantyne could not see the peace being any more than a breathing space. The overweening ambition of Napoleon Bonaparte would never allow him to withdraw meekly from the lists.

He had known William Pitt for a good many years. They were not contemporaries, Pitt being the older by seven years, but their fathers had been friends, so they had at first drifted together, then sought one another out. Both keenly intelligent, they enjoyed sharpening their wits on each other, and each of them played a vicious game of chess, with no quarter given.

He gave a moment's thought to the place where he had expected to be that evening. No doubt by now, Viscount Bradwell would be safe in the bosom of his family, and would already have encountered Mrs Scorer. Had that encounter measured up to expectations, he wondered?

A slight sound behind him roused him from his mood of abstraction, and he turned to see that the valet had now put out his clothes and was clearing his throat discreetly to indicate that it was time to change. One day, Ballantyne mused, as he took off his breeches, but with some caution because of his bruised leg, the army will decide that white trousers are not very sensible; by which time I'll have sold out, no doubt.

Once ready, he returned to the drawing-room where Pitt, who had already changed, was awaiting him. 'Half an hour,' remarked the statesman, consulting his pocket watch, then snapping it shut. 'I'd have expected you to be quicker.'

'So I would have been, had I been prepared to sit down at table in travel-stained linen and a creased coat,' Ballantyne replied.

'I would have thought that campaign life would have taught you to be unconcerned about such things,' said Pitt, indicating by a gesture that they should go together into the dining room.

'Campaign life teaches you many things. One is to distinguish luxuries from necessities,' answered the colonel. 'The other is to enjoy the luxuries when you can get them.'

'Of course. How were things in Egypt, by the way? Were you on Abercrombie's staff for the whole time?'

They chatted about the colonel's experiences in Africa whilst they were being served, and of other matters over dinner, including the property that Ballantyne had recently inherited from his uncle.

At the close of the meal, a servant brought in the bottle which Ballantyne had presented to his host earlier. 'I trust it hasn't suffered,' the colonel said.

Pitt took a sip and smiled appreciatively. 'This is excellent,' he said. 'Come, let's take the rest of it into the drawing room so that we can talk in comfort.'

'Comfort is the last word that I would ever have thought appropriate to use with regard to life in a castle, but this is a snug little place,' the colonel told his host.

'Yes it is, isn't it?' Pitt agreed. 'I like the scale of it. My sister Hester has promised to come and help me remodel the gardens.'

The curtains in the drawing room shut out the dark, adding to the feeling of cosiness, and a small fire burned in the grate, for although it was May, the evening was cool.

The two men sat in silence for a short time, until Pitt said at last, 'You aren't going to ask me, are you?'

'Ask you what?' the colonel replied, one strongly marked dark eyebrow raised quizzically. He sat with one leg, the injured one, stretched out, a glass of port held negligently in long brown fingers.

'Why I invited you.'

'I thought it was a summons rather than an invitation,' said Ballantyne blandly. 'Anyway, I assumed it was to share your birthday. Many happy returns, by the way.' He raised his glass.

Pitt made a dismissive gesture. 'I presume

this lamentable lack of curiosity comes from being obliged to follow orders in the field,' he remarked.

'Oh yes; it's drummed out of us from the very beginning. Besides, you know what curiosity did.'

'You are not a cat and neither am I. Very well, let's finish fencing and get down to business. What do you think of the peace, and more particularly of Addington's administration of it?'

'It won't hold,' Ballantyne replied, his smile disappearing. 'All this heartfelt rejoicing will be found to have come too soon, I fear.'

'Your reasons?'

'Napoleon Bonaparte will never be satisfied with the present state of affairs. He wants to win, and he will not be happy until he is master of all Europe, including this island of ours.'

'And what of Addington?'

Ballantyne got up, limped over to the fire and stood looking down into it. 'I would to God you were still at the helm,' he said. 'Did you know that they're singing a song tonight, written by Canning in your honour? It's entitled 'The Pilot that Weathered the Storm'. Well there's a worse storm ahead and, God help us, we've the wrong pilot to steer us through it.'

Pitt listened impassively, showing no reaction apart from a slight moue of distaste over the matter of the song. 'You know, of course, that he is reducing the size of the army and the navy in order to save money?'

Ballantyne snorted derisively. 'Folly; sheer folly,' he responded. 'Then when war with France becomes inevitable, we will be completely unprepared.'

'Not completely, I trust,' murmured Pitt. 'There is a great deal to be done locally, by way of strengthening defences and organizing volunteers. I have it in mind to set some of that in motion.'

'Please don't tell me that you want me to organize a force of local volunteers,' begged the colonel, his hand up in a defensive gesture.

'Certainly not,' replied Pitt. 'That will give *me* something to think about while I'm here. Being the Warden of the Cinque Ports must needs confer some responsibilities. No, I've an idea that you might be of more use in London.'

'If you've a use for me, then pray tell me,' said the colonel frankly. 'Peace-time soldiering however brief is not to my taste.'

'Don't tell me that you find no pleasure in attending provincial assemblies and attracting the interest of the local squierarchy.'

Ballantyne covered his eyes with his hand. 'Heaven save me,' he uttered. 'I joined the army to serve my country and my king, not to prance about for the edification of onlookers.'

'To serve your country and your king, hmm?' echoed Pitt. 'Just as I'd hoped. I think I may have something for you. I do need to ask about the seriousness of that leg injury, however.'

Ballantyne, who had resumed his seat, gave the said limb a rub. 'It's painful and inconvenient but not serious,' he answered. 'How did you know about it, by the way?'

Pitt permitted himself a small smile. 'I have my sources,' he replied.

'I'm sure you do. What do you have for me?'

'In a moment. Pardon me if I digress a little.' Pitt got up, walked over to the colonel and refilled his glass. 'We've spoken of Bonaparte's ambition. I'm sure you'll agree that life would be very much easier — not to say safer — if he were out of the way.'

'Forgive me, but I thought that that had already been tried,' said Ballantyne drily.

'Yes, it has on a number of occasions, although not as frequently, perhaps, as Napoleon himself would suggest.'

'He exaggerates attempts on his own life?' Ballantyne exclaimed. 'Why the deuce would he want to do such a thing? Is he a madman?'

'Far from it. Sources close to him suggest that he gets a degree of amusement out of frightening his consort. I would imagine that he also likes to stir up hatred against the Jacobins, whom he detests.' Pitt was silent for a moment or two. 'The plot against him that so nearly succeeded was the work of the Royalists of course — with a little help from us.'

'Are you referring to the occasion when he was travelling to a performance of Haydn's *Creation*?' Ballantyne asked.

'On Christmas Eve a couple of years ago,' Pitt agreed.

'Yet you managed to miss Bonaparte and kill fifty others instead,' Ballantyne observed, his tone carefully neutral. 'I hope you don't expect me to be at the sharp end of another attempt.'

'Indeed?' responded Pitt, his brows raised.

'Killing civilians in that kind of underhand way isn't my idea of soldiering at all.'

'You've spoken about your desire to serve your country. All you've done so far is tell me about the things that you're not prepared to do.'

'One of which you said immediately that you didn't want me to do anyway,' the colonel pointed out swiftly. 'Tell me truthfully; do you actually have it in mind for me to go to France and assassinate Napoleon?'

'Would you go if I did?' Pitt asked interestedly.

'One's duty isn't always to one's liking,' Ballantyne observed cynically. 'If you assured me that it was my duty, I'd do it. I don't see how I can go, though, at least not until my leg has healed, and my French, though workman-like, isn't good enough to enable me to pass for a Frenchman.'

'Well calm yourself. I do not have it in mind to make another attempt at present. It's in London that I need you, as I believe I've said already.'

Ballantyne grinned wryly. 'My mother will be pleased. She's been wanting me to dance attendance on her for quite some time.'

'She may get her wish.' He paused. 'We had an agent working for us in London, who was also acting as a double agent in order to mislead the French. A number of people met at her establishment in order to exchange information. We learned a good deal through her. She was one of those sweet old ladies with a mind like a razor.'

Ballantyne frowned. 'You speak of her in the past tense.'

'There's a good reason for that. Recently, she met with an unfortunate accident. Of course, old ladies do fall down the stairs, but our suspicion is that she was pushed in order to prevent her from finding out more.'

'Or from telling you what she had discovered.'

'Indeed. Since then, we believe that the French have moved most of their operations elsewhere. They'd like us to think that they have ceased their activities altogether because of the peace, but it isn't so.'

'They don't believe it will last any more than we do,' Ballantyne agreed.

'No; in Napoleon they have a compelling figurehead to look up to.'

'I'd hazard a guess that Napoleon is proving to be something of a romantic hero,' the colonel suggested. 'His hands are sufficiently clean of the blood from the Terror for him to be attractive to some of the younger émigrés.'

Pitt nodded. 'They believe that he is the man to bring France back to greatness. If they do not think that the peace will hold, then they will do all they can to encourage support for Napoleon whilst our country and France are not upon hostile terms. Naturally, some are seeking to take advantage of the freedom of movement that peace provides in order to improve or re-establish networks of spies. However, that is not the only thing that worries me.'

'Go on.'

'We are not the only ones capable of plotting an assassination,' Pitt explained. 'Were you aware that there was an attempt upon the King's life less than two years ago?'

Ballantyne's eyes narrowed. 'Yes, of course,' he answered. 'Was that not proved to have been the work of some discharged soldier who thought he was God?'

'Indeed. But that does not mean that others will not seek to copy him. He did prove that such a thing was possible, after all. What is more disquieting is that the last message we received from our deceased agent seemed to indicate that such a plot was being planned, and that someone was being sent to carry it out. Unfortunately, we have not learned the identity of the assassin.'

'And you think that the agent may have discovered something and was murdered to keep that discovery secret?'

'Yes, that is my suspicion,' Pitt agreed. 'Of course, a fall on a staircase need not be murder, but the timing of the whole business is rather too good for it to be an accident. I want to discover if our agent was murdered, and if it was because of some specific discovery that she had made. Did the assassins lay their hands on whatever

81

information she might have been trying to protect, and if not, where is it? Is it still in the house? Of course, all of this would not have been necessary had the property not been left in such an inconvenient manner. I had been assured, you see, that it was to pass to the Crown in a roundabout way, and thus we would have been able to put another reliable agent in to take care of things. Instead, I have learned that it has been left to a distant female relative.'

Ballantyne was silent for a short time. 'I am at your disposal. What do you want me to do?'

'I need somebody I can trust to ask a few discreet questions about the old lady's death. While you're there, you might search the place as well.'

'Looking for anything in particular?'

'A code book, which will help us to decipher information about French agents in this country and their plans. It's my belief that our agent was killed either in the hunt for this code book, or because she would not reveal its whereabouts. For this reason, I want you to look after the new owner. Just keep an eye on things, so that if anything untoward occurs, you'll be able to deal with it.'

'I suppose that there is no chance that this heir might be a French agent whom they've managed somehow to inveigle into this position?' asked Ballantyne.

'Most unlikely,' Pitt replied. 'In fact, she's the widow of one of your army officers — a Mrs Scorer.'

'Mrs Scorer!' Ballantyne exclaimed.

'You've heard something?'

'Nothing relevant to this business. I travelled back from Egypt with a connection of hers, that's all. I have her husband's effects to return to her.'

An expression that was almost a smile crept across the statesman's thin features. 'My dear fellow, you have the perfect reason to introduce yourself; that is, unless you have met already?'

'No, I have not met her. Is anything more known about her?'

Pitt picked up a sheet of paper on the table at his elbow. 'She has been living with her cousin roughly for the past two years. She has a son, and until this bequest, she has had no means apart from her army pension. I suppose you know all that already. She may be glad of a man's advice about her new property. I am sure you will find a means of, ah, ingratiating yourself with her.'

'I'm a soldier not a spy, and I have always held back from seducing my officers' widows,' said Ballantyne shortly.

'Seduction may not be necessary; a hand offered in friendship may be sufficient. Have you sold out?'

Ballantyne shook his head. 'I would if I thought that this peace would be lasting,' he admitted. 'I've already told you, peace-time soldiering isn't for me.'

'Your injury to your leg is not permanent, I think you said?'

Ballantyne grimaced. 'No, thank God; just damned inconvenient. There was a problem with the horses onboard ship as we returned from Egypt. I went below to tether one that had broken free and got caught between another horse and the side of the ship. I'm badly bruised, which is why I'm travelling by carriage for the present instead of on horseback, but I'll soon mend.'

Pitt was silent for a moment or two. 'Might I suggest that this injury is, in fact, far more severe, possibly even serious enough for you to have to consider leaving the army? You would then be able to make enquiries much more easily.'

'Not with a seriously injured leg,' Ballantyne pointed out rather mischievously.

'You know what I mean,' replied Pitt. 'A man in uniform is always conspicuous.'

'So is a man of my height,' the colonel suggested.

'You will need to make it clear that you are no longer interested in army matters,' Pitt went on, ignoring the colonel's whimsy. 'Perhaps your wound could have disaffected you in some way. Have you voiced your fears about the brittle nature of this peace to anyone?'

'I'm a soldier,' said Ballantyne again. 'I try to build up morale, not knock it down.'

'Then you could also give the impression that you believe the war is over for good. Court the widow. That way, no one will expect you to be remotely suspicious of anyone.' Pitt got up, took a candle over to a small desk in the window, set it down, took out a sheet of paper, wrote down a few words and handed the paper over. 'This is the name of the place.'

Ballantyne raised his brows. 'Clerkenwell,' he remarked. 'I suppose it was to be expected.'

Pitt nodded. 'Yes, it has ever been something of a hotbed of dissent. There's no doubt that conspiracies have emerged from that area of London, and the people involved with them have gone to ground, but not necessarily gone away.'

'Some were arrested when the law was made more severe,' said Ballantyne. 'I would have thought that the corresponding societies had had their day.'

'One would like to think that they had

all been warned off,' Pitt agreed drily. In the early days of the French Revolution, a number of English radicals had expressed their admiration for the enterprise and had formed groups and societies to discuss how such reform might be achieved in their own country. As the violence in France had increased, so the support for such societies had diminished. But there were still enough of them in existence for the government to be concerned. As Prime Minister, Pitt had presided over a number of laws designed to suppress these clubs and societies. The Treasonable Practices Act and the Seditious Meetings Act, both passed in 1795, followed by the Combination Acts in 1799 had ensured the arrest or at any rate the silence of many traitorous persons, as well as radicals of a much more innocent nature. 'I fear that some of them may still be in operation. More significantly, others may have started up which may prove to be even more dangerous.'

'So I might come across some of those in Clerkenwell,' Ballantyne observed.

'In short, the hotbed of rumour continues.'

'To which I shall be adding, no doubt. How shall I communicate my findings?'

'I'll be in London myself, shortly. I'll be in touch.'

7

Eve had cause to be very grateful to Mr Trafford over the next week, for he visited her almost every day to see how he could be of service. The first thing that he did was discover how serious Eve was about her bookshop.

'What do you know about running a business?' Trafford asked her.

'Not a thing,' Eve responded cheerfully. 'But what can I lose? If I make a disastrous failure of it, I will still have the property to sell at the end of six months, and I might find that I actually enjoy it.'

'There is that,' Trafford agreed cautiously.

'How many servants do you think I ought to have?' Eve asked him.

'You will need a footman,' Trafford began.

'A footman!' exclaimed Eve. 'What on earth would a footman do here? I'm very unlikely to be doing any entertaining, you know.'

'Yes, I know. But a male servant always gives a better look to an establishment and, as you and Miss Sparrow are two women living alone, it will do no harm for the world to see that you have a man to protect you. You cannot always be sure what kind of people may come to your shop, you know.'

'Very well; a footman it is. What else?'

'You need a cook, an abigail, a kitchen maid, and a maid for general cleaning, besides someone to help in the shop.'

'That seems rather a lot,' said Eve thoughtfully. 'I have managed without an abigail for most of my life, you know.'

'Yes, but if you wish to attract any fashionable clients, you will want to look fashionable yourself,' the lawyer pointed out.

'I dare say, but the house is quite small. We will be falling over each other if I employ as many servants as you are suggesting.'

'Believe me, you will find plenty for them all to do, and perhaps they will not all need to live in.'

'I think I must keep the Todds,' Eve said regretfully. 'I did not really take to them, but I cannot reconcile it with my conscience to turn out an old soldier.'

'The woman could be your kitchen maid, or perhaps the general maid, depending on her skills. The man could do odd jobs, although he would not be suitable to be a footman. Do you want me to employ the other servants, or make a selection and send them to you to make a final choice? You ought to choose your own abigail, I think.'

'If I decide that I need one,' Eve reminded him. 'As for the rest, I am sure that I can trust you to find people who will be suitable.'

In the event, Mr Trafford was very fortunate in his quest for servants. The cook was found after an appeal for help from the vicar of St James's. This gentleman had living in his parish a respectable woman whose husband, like Eve's had died on active service.

'Mrs Castle is very capable,' the Vicar said. 'Unfortunately her daughter is a little backward and cannot be left for long periods of time. This makes it hard for Mrs Castle to find employment. She has been taking in sewing, but that is very trying on the eyes.'

'So what is your suggestion?' Trafford asked him.

'The girl, though backward, works perfectly well under her mother's direction,' the vicar told him. 'If Mrs Scorer had the two of them to live in, I believe you would have your cook and kitchen maid in one package, as it were.' As these circumstances were a little unusual, Trafford suggested that Eve might like to go with him to visit Mrs Castle's home to make her own decision.

The soldier's widow lived with her daughter in lodgings in rather a mean-looking dwelling in Ray Street. Although the outside was off-putting in the extreme, the inside was scrupulously clean. Mrs Castle, a slight, careworn-looking woman, aged beyond her years, was dressed plainly, but very neatly, as was her daughter, a wispy looking girl of about 12 or 13. Eve thought that she looked not so much backward as painfully shy.

Rather diffidently, Mrs Castle invited her unexpected visitors to partake of a cup of tea and biscuits. The tea was of poor quality, but the biscuits, homemade and slightly warm, though plain were excellent, and Eve's mind was made up. Mrs Castle and Joanna would be installed the very next day.

There were tears in the good woman's eyes as she waved her visitors off at the door. 'This is the first bit of good luck I've had since I lost my Billy,' she said.

Mr Trafford gave a lot of thought to the selection of a footman. He was well aware that the man he chose would set the tone for the whole establishment. It was vitally important, therefore, that his character should be good, and this was certainly not the case as far as all London footmen were concerned. Fortunately, while he was still thinking about this matter, a colleague informed him of a likely man, a former soldier, who was looking for a position, and came with an excellent recommendation from his commanding officer. The lawyer arrived at Clerkenwell Green with his news just as dinner was about to be served and apologized for his clumsy timing.

'Not at all,' Eve replied. 'I have discovered that we keep country hours, and that five is quite early to be dining in London these days. Is it too early for your meal, or would you like to join us?'

Once reassured that he would not be intruding, Mr Trafford, a childless widower who lived alone, accepted with pleasure, and he was soon telling her over an excellent dinner — cooked by Mrs Castle — that he thought he had found the very man.

'This peace favours us,' he said, as they sat at table with Miss Sparrow. 'The prime minister is reducing the size of the army and the navy, so there are some good men looking for work. The man who will be coming here — Goodman by name, strangely enough — comes very highly recommended by his former commanding officer.'

'I want him to open the door, not round up the enemy,' Eve protested.

'I am sure you will find him useful for all kinds of other things, my dear Eve,' remarked Miss Sparrow, for the ladies were now upon Christian-name terms.

Trafford smiled. 'You are very right, Miss Sparrow,' he said approvingly. 'I did warn him that he would have to be prepared to turn his hand to anything. Who will move those heavy boxes of books about, for instance? Or mend the window catch if it goes? I respect your reasons for retaining Todd, but do not try to tell me that you will be able to depend upon him for anything.'

The only matter still to be dealt with was the question of help in the shop. 'I wouldn't worry too much about it, if I were you,' Trafford said reassuringly. 'The stipulation was that you should keep the business open. Nothing was said about *how* open it should be, or how successful. You could quite easily open just one morning a week and if it runs at a loss, what does it matter? You will have fulfilled the terms of the will.'

Eve agreed politely that it would be so. Secretly, however, she was determined to do rather more than simply prevent the place from falling down. She had never really had an establishment of her own before. The house in which she had lived with her mother and father had been small, and after her mother's death, her father had not wanted anything to be changed. Edmund's parents' home, to which she had gone after her marriage, had never been hers to do with as she wished. Now, finding herself the mistress of a property which comprised both home and business, her mind began whirling with countless possibilities.

She refused to be daunted. Although she had never dreamed of running a business before, she had a good head for figures, and was used to keeping accounts. She was also accustomed to organizing a household. Surely those skills would stand her in good stead? The challenge would make a welcome change to that posed by the need to keep her cousin in a good mood!

The morning after Trafford had dined with them, therefore, she sat at her desk in the drawing room making a list of the things that needed to be done in order to prepare the bookshop and library for use.

i   Check files for unreturned books.
ii   Make sure books are in order on shelves
iii Make myself familiar with stock
iv   Dust and tidy bookshop and library
v   Ask Goodman to clean windows
vi   Visit Hatchard's to spy

She looked at the last item on her list and by dint of a rather convoluted reasoning process, she decided that it ought to go at the top.

She and Miss Sparrow had popped in to

Hatchard's in Piccadilly at the end of a shopping expedition that the older lady had insisted upon. Eve had been dubious of the necessity. 'I shall be living a very quiet life here among my books,' she had said. 'I do not anticipate the need to cut a dash. Besides, I am still in mourning.'

'My dear Eve,' Miss Sparrow had replied, 'Mr Trafford has already told you that you need to be ready to welcome fashionable people to your shop. You will not wish to look like a dowd in front of them, I am sure, mourning or no mourning. If I do not make certain that you visit Mlle le Brun, then I shall consider that I have failed in my responsibilities.'

Eve had agreed, but not without some trepidation. It had been years since she had had anything new that she had not made herself, and if she were completely honest, she felt a little intimidated at the idea of visiting a fashionable modiste. But with Miss Sparrow's support and surprisingly commanding manner at Mlle le Brun's, the result had been that she had come home with a number of boxes and packages, together with the understanding that she would return to Conduit Street for a final fitting. She decided to go to the modiste then reward herself for her patience with a visit to Hatchard's afterwards.

After a brief reflection, she determined to go alone. Miss Sparrow was needed to look after Luke, since a nursemaid had not yet been found, and in any case, Eve wanted to be able to look round Hatchard's undisturbed, without drawing attention to herself, or worrying that she was keeping someone else waiting. 'You will be quite safe with Goodman to look after you,' said Miss Sparrow.

'Very true,' Eve replied blandly. She could, of course, have instructed Goodman to go with her, she reflected guiltily, as she set off alone in a hackney. That would have meant that he would not be able to clean the windows, though, another task on her list. After all, it was only a short walk from Mlle le Brun's to Hatchard's.

The fact of the matter was that having spent a year under her cousin's eye and pandering to her whims, she now welcomed the chance to make her own decisions, and escape scrutiny. She could not remember when she had last felt so free.

Faithful to her promise on the previous visit, the little dressmaker had prepared everything that Eve had ordered, and the latter was very pleased to discover that the gowns that had been cut out for her fitted her very well. To her surprise, *Madame* seemed very far from satisfied and the visit took much longer than Eve had expected. She was bound to acknowledge, however, that after what seemed like a lifetime of living in Cousin Julia's hand-me-downs, it was very gratifying to wear colours and fashions of her own choosing. Eventually she emerged from the modiste's feeling as if she had been pushed, pinned and measured as much as a woman could stand, and she was longing for a sit down and perhaps a cup of coffee.

There were numerous coffee and chocolate houses in London, she knew. She and Miss Sparrow had passed some of them and had not gone in although she had seen ladies inside them as well as gentlemen. She had a suspicion that she ought to have an escort, but there was none; it was no use repining, and meantime she was feeling parched. Besides, she told herself stoutly, she was not a slip of a girl: she was a businesswoman of twenty-five years of age, and a widow.

She paused outside a coffee shop called Russell's that looked quiet and respectable. She opened the door and went inside and noted that there was an alcove towards the back that was unoccupied. She decided that this would be an appropriately secluded spot for a lady on her own. She took her place and realized at once that a waiter had noted her presence. Since the place was quiet, she naturally expected that she would soon be served. Instead, she saw him look at her with an unmistakably anxious expression on his face, then cross the room to confer with a neatly dressed man, who looked at her in his turn. Then, after a moment's hesitation, this man came over to speak to her and, to her astonishment, suggested that she might like to leave.

'Oh dear, are you about to close?' she asked, thinking of the amount of time that she had spent in the modiste's. She had not thought that it was so late. Indeed, she had supposed that after a cup of coffee here she would still have time to look in at Hatchard's.

No, they were not closing, the man replied, but he was sure that she would be more comfortable elsewhere, and again suggested that she should leave straight away.

'I can assure you that I am perfectly comfortable here,' Eve replied, her eye kindling. 'There appears to be plenty of room and I am very thirsty. Is my custom not good enough for you, sir?'

The proprietor — for Eve assumed that the man must be he — opened his mouth to speak again. Before he could do so, the door opened and a group of six or seven men came in, laughing and talking. Suddenly, from seeming quite empty, the room began to feel rather full.

'Russell! Where the deuce are you?' one of the men demanded.

With a brief bow in her direction, Mr Russell — for it was indeed he — hurried to greet his new customers, but one of them, seeing where he was, and detecting Eve's presence in the alcove, exclaimed, 'Stap me, but he's provided a wench for us! Dashed good of you, Russell.'

'If you've any energy for wenching after a few rounds at Jackson's, then you're a better man than I am,' declared another.

Eve recalled seeing Jackson's boxing saloon when she had been out shopping with Miss Sparrow. Clearly, these men had made an arrangement to come here after taking exercise. That was what Russell must have been trying to tell her a few moments ago.

'Well, I *am* a better man,' answered the first of the group, walking towards the alcove, where Eve had now got to her feet. He was of medium height and slender, quite good-looking with dark-blond hair brushed into a Brutus, and rather sharp features.

'Forgive me,' Eve said. 'I did not realize that these places were taken. I will bid you good day, gentlemen.'

'No need to be unfriendly,' said another of the men. He was a little stouter than his companion and looked to be several years older. 'We're happy to share.' Between them, these two men were blocking her exit.

'Thank you, but I would like to leave now, if you please,' said Eve, her voice still firm, she was glad to note, even though her heart was beating rather rapidly. Surely she could not be ravished in a coffee shop on New Bond Street in broad daylight?

'But you can't,' said the blond man. 'Not without your escort.'

Eve opened her mouth to say that she had no escort, a fact which she was sure they had guessed already, then realized that she would be walking into a trap. How she wished that she had not come in here, however thirsty she might be. If only she had had Goodman to wait by her chair and show that she was a person of some standing. Heavens! They clearly supposed her to be a woman of the streets!

The blond man gave a low laugh. 'Oh dear,' he said.

Suddenly, another voice spoke from behind the group. 'Are you ready, ma'am? I'm sorry for the delay but I was unavoidably detained.'

At the sound of his voice, the group parted to reveal a very tall, broad gentleman with dark hair and striking features. He was dressed in military uniform.

Eve only hesitated for a split second. Denial would leave her at the mercy of these rogues, whereas if she went with him and he happened to be evil-intentioned, then she would at least have only one man to deal with.

Whilst Edmund had been in the army, she had made it her business to familiarize herself with the dress and ranks of regiments of the British Army, and of cavalry regiments in particular. She was therefore able to take one swift look at her would-be rescuer's uniform and say confidently, 'Thank you, Colonel. I am quite ready.'

The colonel was not quite finished, however. 'These gentlemen will wish to take . . . ah . . . appropriate leave of you, no doubt.'

Suddenly the mood of the throng had become respectful rather than raucous. 'Of course,' said the blond man, bowing politely. 'Good day, ma'am, and our apologies for having startled you.'

'You are very kind,' Eve replied rather stiffly. 'Good day, sir.'

With a nod to Russell, Eve's escort opened the door and followed her out. 'I believe I owe you my thanks, sir,' she said, as soon as they were clear of the coffee shop. As she turned towards him, she saw that he walked rather stiffly and leaned heavily upon a cane.

'Yes, I think you do,' was the rather disconcerting reply. 'But I think you also owe me an explanation, ma'am.' His expression, she noted, was hard and uncompromising.

'An explanation?' she replied, lifting her chin a little.

He looked at her curiously for a moment or two before saying, 'There must be a reason why someone who is obviously a lady — or at any rate appears to be one — should be sitting on her own in a coffee house so close to Jackson's boxing saloon.'

'My business is my own,' Eve replied, colouring a little. His suggestion that she might only *look* like a lady infuriated her; then she remembered thinking that the men in Russell's had come to just that conclusion.

'Forgive me, ma'am, I was obliged to make it mine just a few minutes ago,' replied the colonel in the same unbending tone.

'You were not obliged to do any such thing,' Eve retorted.

'Oh, indeed. What about my obligation as a gentleman to a lady in distress? Would you prefer that I took you back to join those charming gentlemen in Russell's?' he asked, catching hold of her arm. 'There did not appear to me to be quite enough seats around the table, but I'm sure that one of them will allow you to sit on his knee, if you ask nicely.' For a moment, it almost seemed as if he intended to drag her back inside Russell's.

Eve shook him off, drawing herself up to her full height. 'Unhand me, sir!' she exclaimed. 'No, I would not prefer. I have already thanked you for your intervention. I acknowledge that you played a gentleman's part, and thanks should be all that an officer and a gentleman requires under such circumstances.' She emphasized the word 'gentleman' slightly and had the satisfaction of seeing the man draw his brows together.

'Very well, ma'am, I will say no more,' he answered. Then immediately he contradicted himself by going on to state, 'You are clearly from the provinces with no idea of how to go on in London. Let me inform you that ladies who wish to retain their reputations do not walk alone in Town, nor do they go into coffee shops unescorted, and especially not that one at that time of day. I'm surprised Russell did not warn you.' Eve's gaze flickered away from his as she recalled the proprietor's well-meaning attempts to persuade her to leave. The military gentleman, seeing this, said ironically, 'Just so, ma'am.

Now, is there any way in which I may serve you further?'

Eve was on the point of answering with a decided negative when the chiming of a nearby clock alerted her to the time. She would not be able to spend any time at Hatchard's today. 'Will you summon a hackney for me, if you please?'

With an irritatingly small amount of effort, the colonel did as she asked, and when the carriage stopped, he bowed politely. 'You see how much of a gentleman I am,' he remarked. 'I'm not even going to attempt to overhear your address.'

As he stepped back, she became aware once more that he was very lame, and she was suddenly stricken with guilt because of her ungracious behaviour towards one of the country's heroes. 'May I set you down anywhere, sir?' she asked him impulsively.

For the first time, that granite-like countenance softened, and across his features there appeared an expression of genuine amusement. 'You are very good,' he said politely, 'but you don't really know me well enough to be alone with me in a closed carriage, do you?'

'Odious man!' she muttered under her breath, before giving her direction and climbing inside.

Ballantyne beckoned to a young lad who was loitering nearby, and handed him a coin and one of his cards. 'Find out where that lady is going, then come back and tell me. Don't let her see you.'

'Yes, guv!'

The colonel stood and watched the carriage depart, the boy racing after it, then taking advantage of a brief halt to the traffic by jumping up and clinging to the back like a monkey.

Newly arrived in London, Ballantyne had wandered into Russell's by chance, and had intervened from motives of disinterested chivalry. When she had looked straight at him outside the coffee house, he had thought that he had recognized her. Then when he had seized hold of her arm and she had glared at him, he had realized that he was face to face for the first time with Eve Scorer. The bonnet had confused him at first, which was why he had not recognized her immediately.

What had she been doing in Russell's? He had heard that she might be careless of her reputation. This latest incident seemed to confirm his worst fears. Of course, it was not really any of his business how she chose to conduct herself. She was not related to him, and Captain Scorer was not alive to be concerned about his wife's behaviour. But for a long time now, the army, the regiment, had been his family, and Eve, if only by adoption, was part of it. Even if Edmund Scorer had not commended her to his care, he would still feel a sense of responsibility towards her. Furthermore, a woman who was careless about her loyalty to her husband might be similarly careless about her loyalty to her country.

Nevertheless in thinking about today's encounter, he found himself admiring her. He remembered the way in which she had shaken off his hand, and stared up at him fearlessly, even though he was the taller by at least a foot. Despite himself, he grinned wryly. Many people, he found, were intimidated by his height and bearing; Mrs Scorer was clearly not one of them. The one thing that he must never forget, however, was the task with which he had been entrusted by William Pitt. Part of that involved looking after this woman. This very afternoon, he had not only been given an opportunity to put her under an obligation to him, but he had also been able to observe her when she was off guard. Perhaps it was a good omen for the future of his mission.

8

The day after Eve had departed for London, Julia was delighted to receive a call from Horace Bunty. She had been attracted to the younger of the Bunty sons soon after her arrival in the area as a new bride three years before. Her marriage to Neville Comberton had been one founded upon expediency rather than affection, at least on her side. She had not relished moving to the countryside, for she had been born and brought up in Bath, and Neville, a countryman to his fingertips, had immersed himself in country pursuits, forgetting that his young wife might need entertaining.

Horace Bunty had stepped into the breach with alacrity. A little dalliance with a married woman suited him well, for he had no desire to saddle himself with the commitments that a marriage of his own would entail. As far as he was concerned, his brother Jeremy was welcome to negotiate a protracted, delicate courtship with the vicar's commonplace daughter. The opportunity to flirt with, kiss, and fondle his neighbour's wife was far more to his taste.

This delightful pastime was curtailed somewhat during Julia's pregnancy and immediately after her lying-in. Then, when young Master Thomas was only a matter of months old, his father took a very bad tumble from his horse and died some weeks later. Julia went very properly into black and, for appearances, if not because of her own inclination, ceased to receive male callers.

Bunty was quite sanguine about the whole business. Although he found Julia very desirable, there were plenty of other women who were ready to succumb to his style of blond handsomeness.

Julia, however, found herself with a dilemma. For the sake of propriety, she needed to find someone to live with her, but there was no one whose name immediately sprang to mind. Then she received a letter from her cousin Eve, asking for help. This was the perfect solution to her problems. Eve's presence would answer the demands of propriety, but because Eve was not in any position to dictate terms, Julia would not feel bound to pay her as she would any other companion. Nobody else would want to employ a woman with a small child in tow. Eve would therefore be obliged to turn a blind eye to any questionable activity of her hostess, if she did not want to be out on her ear.

So Eve arrived at Stonecrop House and settled in. Now adequately chaperoned, Julia was able to receive visitors of both sexes, and in due course of time, Horace Bunty came to call. Then the most unexpected and, for Eve, unwelcome eventuality arose: Bunty transferred his interest from the one widow to the other.

Quite why he did so, both ladies would have found it impossible to say. On the surface, Julia was far more conventionally beautiful, and she knew it. Why would any man be attracted by light-brown hair, sherry-coloured eyes, a trim figure and a determined chin, when he could look at dusky curls, melting blue eyes, and voluptuous curves? Furthermore, Julia's idea of mourning attire was shimmering grey, spotless white, or deep, lustrous black, all ornamented with rich lace, and enhanced with pearls or diamonds. Eve, on the other hand, wore unadorned, plain gowns of bombazine, and eschewed jewellery apart from her wedding ring and a simple gold locket which had been given to her by her husband.

In common with many rakes, however, Mr Bunty had a tendency to scorn what was available to him and covet what appeared to be out of his reach. Julia indicated to him, oh so discreetly, that she would be happy to take up where they had left off. Eve, on the other hand, treated him with polite distance, and then with repulsive coldness when he began to show an interest in her, and consequently he became intrigued.

Unsurprisingly, perhaps, gallantry towards married women was not the only vice in which Bunty indulged. An unsuccessful period of gambling led to debts which his father was hard put to it to settle, and in an effort to separate him from his bad habits, Mr Bunty made arrangements for his younger son to go to Jamaica to oversee some property there.

For Eve, his departure came at just the right time. He had managed to corner her on one or two occasions, without serious consequences, and Julia, although a little puzzled that he was holding back from her, did not suspect that he could possibly prefer her cousin, so Eve had remained.

Julia had been delighted at his return from the West Indies. He had acquired a healthy-looking tan and, as far as she was concerned, he looked more attractive than ever. For his part, Bunty had been mingling with some very exotic beauties whilst overseas, and Julia reminded him of several of them. Eve, on the other hand, now in grey, and still with that air of hauteur, came as a refreshing contrast, and he was even more determined to pursue her.

On the evening of Julia's dinner party, desire, together with a liberal consumption of wine, had made him reckless, and he had pounced upon Eve at the foot of the stairs, regardless of who might come upon them. It had been the very worst of bad luck that Julia had appeared, but at least she had seemed inclined to put the blame onto Eve for encouraging him.

He did not want to alienate Julia by any means. Her husband had left her in comfortable circumstances and she was a member of the Earl of Wirksworth's family. It would not do to get on the wrong side of such a powerful landowner. What was more, he might yet decide to marry her for his prudish grandmother had withdrawn his allowance following his bad behaviour. He had written her a letter the following day, therefore, hinting in the subtlest way that he had been overcome by drink, and Eve had taken advantage of him.

He had intended to follow up his letter with a call, but a nasty cold laid him low for a few days, and while not a man to coddle himself, he had no intention of appearing before either Julia, or Eve, with a red nose and streaming eyes.

As soon as he was well enough, he rode over to Stonecrop House, and was not a little relieved at the charming welcome he was given when he was shown into the back parlour which faced onto the garden. His relief made him behave more affectionately toward Julia than he had done since his return, and before very much time had passed, she was cosily ensconced upon his knee.

'I knew you couldn't possibly be really interested in Eve,' she said confidently, between kisses.

'I told you in my letter, I drank too much wine and when she led me on, I couldn't resist,' he answered, smiling, wondering the while how much struggling Eve would put up before he could get her in a similar position.

'All those army wives are just camp-followers,' she said with a blithe disregard for the truth. 'Well, thank goodness I am rid of her now.'

If Bunty had not been in the very act of nuzzling her neck, he might have given himself away by the expression on his face. As it was, he paused infinitesimally in what he was doing, then said in a carefully uninterested tone, 'Did you turn her off?' Eve

Scorer, homeless and with very few resources, might be glad of a protector, he mused.

'No, for she has come into property.'

'Lucky for her.'

'She'll have to get her hands grubby in trade, though. Apparently, the house comes with a shop attached — in Clerkenwell, of all places.'

'I don't suppose she'll mind that,' Bunty answered, baring Julia's shoulder and pressing a kiss upon it. 'She's not such a lady as you, my dear.'

Pleased with this response, Julia allowed him further liberties, unaware that he was already plotting how to get to London.

★   ★   ★

Five days later, his father provided him with the perfect excuse. There was business to be dealt with by their man of affairs at Temple Bar. Either Horace or Jeremy would have to go, and Horace willingly volunteered.

By this time, Julia had actually become his mistress, and he knew that he would have to bid her farewell, at least for the time being. He took himself into Sheffield, therefore, to buy her a bracelet as a parting gift, and rode over to break the news.

He was a little behind the times. His

mother had paid a visit to Mrs Comberton already, and had informed Julia of her son's imminent departure. Having got what she wanted, Julia had no intention of allowing Bunty to escape, and although she was not a little annoyed that he had made his plans without reference to her, she was determined not to let him know it. Finding a letter from her brother-in-law which stated that he was going to be returning home, she decided to go to London in order to meet him there. Horace, therefore, found her full of her own plans for a removal to London, and with exclamations of what a happy coincidence it was that they would be able to travel together. Bunty found himself obliged to agree.

★   ★   ★

Jason Ballantyne was coming away from Angelo's fencing academy in no very good mood. His encounter with Eve had reminded him of occasions when he and her late husband had fenced together. Having met the boy who had followed Eve and discovered, as he had expected, that she had gone straight to Clerkenwell, he had wandered into the academy, thinking that he would have an opportunity to chat with acquaintances about old times. He had reckoned without how frustrating it would feel, for he was obliged to watch other men sparring whilst he stood back, kept from joining in by the need to maintain the fiction that he and Pitt had created.

He was in great need of cheering up, so his heart lifted when he saw a carriage pulled up at the side of the road, with Captain Lord Bradwell talking to its occupant. He limped over to offer a greeting, and the broad grin with which Bradwell welcomed his advent told him that the feeling of pleasure was entirely mutual.

'In a good hour,' Bradwell exclaimed. 'M'dear fellow, come and be introduced to m'sister-in-law!'

'With the greatest pleasure,' Ballantyne responded. 'I thought you were going to Sheffield.'

'So I am,' agreed Bradwell, 'but when I discovered that Julia was in town, I decided to pay her my respects before travelling on to see m'father. Julia, my dear, this is Colonel Jason Ballantyne, hero of the Egyptian campaign. Jason, meet m'sister, Mrs Comberton.'

Ballantyne, raising his eyes to the occupant of the barouche, saw the most enchantingly pretty woman that he had set eyes on for a long time. 'Colonel Ballantyne,' she murmured, holding out her hand. 'What can I say, except that I salute you?'

'You can disbelieve most of what Bradwell says for a start, ma'am,' he answered, raising her hand to his lips. 'I'm no more of a hero than any man who fought for his country.'

'But you are wounded,' she murmured. 'That makes you exceedingly gallant, surely.'

'It makes him exceedingly foolhardy,' Bradwell put in. 'Fortunately — '

Fearful of what the other man might say with regard to the extent of his injuries, Ballantyne said quickly, 'Fortunately no one else was injured in the incident. I fear that my soldiering days are done, however.'

'Done?' exclaimed Bradwell. 'Good God, man, are you sure?'

'That is what the doctor says,' Ballantyne assured him.

'How horrid,' shuddered Mrs Comberton. 'Please say no more about it!'

'With the greatest of pleasure, ma'am,' Ballantyne responded promptly. He had no desire whatsoever to prolong the conversation and give Bradwell the opportunity to ask for further information about his injury. He recalled Mrs Scorer's assistance, albeit offered unwisely, and wondered fleetingly whether the officer's widow would react as her cousin had done.

'I have just been asking Andrew to dine with me this evening. Would you care to join

115

us if you are not engaged elsewhere? As long as you do not talk about fighting, or injuries, or anything horrid.'

'I should be delighted,' Ballantyne replied. He had only returned to London that day, and had had the intention of dining at home with his mother. Enquiries at his house in Berkeley Square, however, had elicited the information that Mrs Ballantyne and her niece were going to a ball on the outskirts of London and would not be returning until very late. Furthermore, it also occurred to him that dinner with Mrs Scorer's cousin might be another way of furthering his relationship with Mrs Scorer herself.

★　★　★

Julia was very pleased that evening by the splendid effect created by two tall, striking gentlemen arriving at her house in uniform. Unfortunately, although it was not dark when they arrived, they came by carriage, owing to Colonel Ballantyne's injury, and the rest of the street was thus denied the spectacle of the colonel and the captain striding up to her front door. She did instruct her butler to wait to answer the door for as long as courtesy permitted, to give her neighbours the maximum chance of observing that there was someone intimately acquainted with not one but two of England's heroes living in the street.

Her impression of Colonel Ballantyne when she had met him in Bond Street had been mixed, for his uniform, although superficially dashing, had been somewhat travel-stained. This evening, however, his appearance was immaculate and did not suggest that he could not afford to replace his clothing should the need arise. That disposed of one tiny fear. She certainly did not want to find some half-pay officer forever on the doorstep, looking for a free meal, however powerfully masculine he might be. The good impression that he made was confirmed by a very brief conversation which revealed that he was the owner of a house in Berkeley Square as well as a neat estate in Hampshire.

For his part, Jason Ballantyne was favourably impressed with Julia Comberton, although his approval was tempered with caution. On the one hand, her style of curvaceous prettiness appealed to him, and her gracious manner was very welcoming. His senses, assailed as they had been by the sights and sounds of an army camp and military campaigns, were soothed by her smiles, and by every aspect of the home over which he assumed she presided, but which was in fact organized by a very efficient housekeeper.

On the other hand, there was something about her which reminded him of the friend of his mother who had seduced him when he was seventeen. Mrs Comberton was not to blame for that, but the very likeness made him cautious.

They sat down four to dinner, the two gentlemen, Mrs Comberton, and a faded, depressed-looking lady who was introduced as 'Miss Pewtress, my companion.'

'It is very good of you to entertain a stranger, ma'am,' Ballantyne told his hostess in his rather deep voice as they sat at dinner.

'I should think myself failing in my duty if I did not give succour to one of England's heroes,' Julia replied, with pretty courtesy.

'You already have a hero in your own family,' the colonel observed, after a short pause.

'We are very proud of Bradwell,' Julia agreed, smiling at her brother-in-law, who responded by raising his glass.

'Of course,' the colonel agreed politely. 'But I was referring to Captain Scorer. I believe that you had his widow living with you until very recently.' He was watching Julia carefully as he spoke, and noted a shadow cross her face.

'Yes, she did live with me, and a vast deal

of inconvenience she has caused me,' Julia replied, in a rather peevish tone.

'I'm sorry to hear that, ma'am,' the colonel said politely. 'I have never met the lady, but I knew her husband well.'

'I am sure that he was all that you say,' responded Julia, 'but his wife was not very fair to me — or to Horace Bunty, for that matter.'

'Horace Bunty,' Bradwell murmured. 'Would that be the younger son of the people who live at the Limes?'

'That is so,' his sister-in-law agreed. 'Her efforts to intrigue herself with him would have been very embarrassing if they were not laughable. Why, at my last dinner party she was so busy dallying at the foot of the stairs that she forgot to fetch help for a sick woman. I would have been obliged to dismiss her had she not left of her own accord.'

'Surely one only dismisses a servant,' Ballantyne responded quickly, before he had properly thought about the matter. Unconsciously, he was using almost the same phrase as Eve had used before she left Stonecrop House.

As if realizing that she had gone too far, Julia smiled brightly, and said, 'Silly me, I am boring you with my domestic arrangements, am I not? Is your mother in London for the

119

season, Colonel Ballantyne?'

Later, after he had returned home, Jason gave some thought to the position of Eve Scorer in her cousin's household, and about the character of the woman whom he was bound in honour to visit.

Obviously Julia Comberton resented her cousin. Could it simply be because Eve had behaved badly towards Horace Bunty, a neighbour, or were there other reasons?

9

Clearly Eve's visit to Hatchard's would demand an expedition all its own, but her unfortunate experience had given her a distaste for the fashionable part of town, at least for the time being. She decided, therefore, to spend a few days in the bookshop and library, establishing what was there and finding any catalogues or lists of stock that there might be. Fortunately, Mme Lascelles seemed to have kept reasonably accurate records.

Goodman had settled in very quickly. He was a stocky man of medium height, with sandy hair, an upright stance, and a direct bright blue gaze and he had a blunt way with him that Eve found very reassuring.

It transpired that literacy was one of Goodman's accomplishments and he very willingly agreed to check the stock in the bookshop against Mme Lascelles' list whilst she, Eve, checked the books in the library. The task took two or three days, and also involved some dusting as well as counting and checking, but at the end of that time, she felt quite confident that she had a good idea of what was on her shelves. She also had a list of books that had been borrowed, together with the names of those who had them in their possession, with their addresses recorded in a separate place. She would write to these people, informing them that the establishment would be opening again soon, so that they could return their books and, with any luck, borrow more.

The following day, she decided, she would go to Hatchard's to spy out the land. She would also deliver two of her letters. One was for a Miss Mirfield who lived in Berkeley Square and who had two items on loan; a book of poems by Mr Southey, and a novel entitled *The Memoirs of Emma Courtney* by Mary Hays. The other letter was for a Mr Harpin whose address was in Ryder Street. She dared say that a certain obnoxious military gentleman might think she was very green, but she knew better than to visit an address of what clearly must be bachelor lodgings, which could only be approached by walking down St James's, where everyone knew that the gentlemen's clubs were to be found.

This time, she decided, she would avail herself of Goodman's escort. Miss Sparrow would remain at home to keep an eye on Luke. The one member of staff whom Eve had not yet succeeded in recruiting had been someone to look after her son. She was very particular about the person who would eventually be entrusted with this task, and was in no hurry to employ anyone unless she was very sure of that person's capabilities. Fortunately, Miss Sparrow, who after one visit to her sister had kept well away from her relative, very willingly took on this role. 'He is old enough to begin formal schooling,' that lady had remarked, 'and when he does so, a governess had better be employed. For now, he is happy with me, and there is no need to rush. I never had the opportunity to marry and have children of my own, you know, and I enjoy his company.'

For the occasions when Eve needed Miss Sparrow to be her chaperon, Mrs Castle declared that she would be very happy to look after Luke. 'He's a likely lad,' she said. 'Like his papa, is he?'

'Yes, very like,' Eve agreed. Indeed, Luke was growing apace and would need new breeches before he had even begun to wear out his first pair. It gave her another reason to be thankful for the extra income.

She was pleased that on the very morning when she had planned to make this expedition, one of her walking dresses was delivered from Mlle le Brun. It was a charming, high-waisted gown of lilac with silvery grey lace, with a spencer of a darker shade and a bonnet with matching ribbons. She had had to admit that she had felt a little outmoded on her previous visit to the fashionable quarter. No wonder the military gentleman had been able to detect that she was from the provinces. Well this time, no one would be able to find fault with her appearance!

Before going downstairs, she paused at the top of the flight. She reflected guiltily that she had given very little thought to the fate of her kinswoman who had died in this very house. Now, she wondered whether this might be the very spot from which she had fallen. She looked down. There were no loose portions of carpet in which one might catch a foot, and the floor was not so highly polished for someone to slip. Perhaps Mme Lascelles *had* suddenly become faint. As Eve came downstairs, she reflected that she would have to ask Biddy Todd if she or her husband had found the old lady, or if it had been some other servant who had now left. After all, the house was accessible from the shop, and anyone might have come in at the crucial moment.

She had just given Goodman instructions to procure a hackney and was glancing

124

around the library and imagining it being visited by Miss Mirfield and Mr Harpin, among others, when there was a knock at the door. Because Goodman was out and there was no one else nearby, Eve opened the door herself, to find a slight young man with silvery fair hair and a diffident expression standing in front of her.

'I am very sorry, sir, but I fear that the shop and the library are not yet open, although I hope that they will be very soon. How may I assist you?'

'Good morning,' replied the young man with a shy smile. 'I beg your pardon, *madame*, for intruding in this unmannerly way, but I live nearby and did a little work for Mme Lascelles by way of serving in the shop and in the library. I was wondering whether you too might similarly need assistance?' His English was faultless, but a slight accent betrayed his origins.

'Pray step inside for a few moments,' said Eve, very conscious that she had not yet found anyone to work in the shop. 'I can tell that you are French. Were you perhaps a connection of M. Lascelles?'

He shook his head. 'I did not have that honour,' he replied. 'Allow me to introduce myself. I am Aristide D'Angers, and my family were landowners in France. We lost

125

our property in the Revolution and many of my family perished on the guillotine. I am obliged to find work in order to support myself and my invalid mother.'

'I am Eve Scorer and I do most sincerely pity you and your situation,' said Eve in sympathetic tones. 'However, you must forgive me if I do not commit myself at present, as I am on the point of going out. Would you be so good as to call tomorrow with perhaps some form of reference so that I may consider your request?'

'*Merci, madame*,' D'Angers replied, bowing as he left.

Eve thought about the young Frenchman as she and Goodman travelled into town. Was he as honest and straightforward as he seemed? True, England and France were not at war at present, although that state of affairs could surely not last for long. Furthermore, there were many French people who did not approve of Napoleon and his tactics, and D'Angers could be one of them. What was more, she certainly needed assistance with her stock. Out of idle curiosity, she asked Goodman's opinion.

'You do need someone to help in the shop, ma'am,' he replied. 'Why not take the man on for a short trial, and see how you like him?'

'Thank you, Goodman,' Eve replied, in a

tone of real gratitude. 'I believe I may.'

Eve had already decided that whilst Goodman took the letter to Ryder Street on foot, she would take the other to Berkeley Square, an address where hopefully no boxing habitués would be found. Then she would travel the short distance to Piccadilly and meet Goodman at Hatchard's so that he could escort her home.

The hackney carriage dropped Goodman at the top of St James's Street, then took Eve to Berkeley Square, where she instructed the driver to wait for her once he had discovered where Miss Mirfield lived. The day was bright and sunny, and she would very much have liked a walk, but she did not want to attract any unwelcome attention, especially from any gentlemen who might have been frequenting boxing establishments!

She knocked firmly on the front door and when the butler answered it, she gave him the letter with a civil request that it should be handed to Miss Mirfield. That done, she climbed back into the hackney, which then began the short journey to Hatchard's in Piccadilly. The carriage had only just started to move when out of the corner of her eye, Eve saw a figure approaching the house that she had just left. He was no longer in military uniform, but there was no mistaking his tall figure, the rather halting gait and the walking cane. It was the officious gentleman who had rescued her from Russell's and then lectured her about her behaviour.

She sat back quickly, turning her face away. What a blessing that he had not arrived in time to find her leaving the house! There was a chance that he might be a relative of Miss Mirfield. Eve had been delighted to find that she had a customer living at such a fashionable address. The last thing that she wanted was for some connection of her customer to decide that Mrs Scorer was not a respectable person from whom to borrow books!

10

'Is that a note for me?' Colonel Ballantyne asked the butler, seeing in the man's hand the very missive that Eve had just delivered. He had left the house earlier in the day and had just returned.

'No, sir, it's for Miss Victoria.'

'I'll take it to her. Thank you, Cray.' He left his hat with the butler, and made his way into the drawing room, the note in his hand. The room was already occupied by two ladies, one lying on a *chaise-longue*, the other standing in front of the empty fireplace in a walking dress and bonnet.

'You see,' said the lady who was lying down. 'Jason has come home, and most fortuitously. He will take you.'

'Good morning, Mama,' responded Ballantyne, crossing to where his parent was lying, and lifting to his lips the hand which she extended to him.

'My poor, wounded son,' sighed Mrs Ballantyne. 'Crippled in the service of his country. You should not be going out on your own like this.'

Ballantyne made no response to this

speech, apart from a bow and a slight frown of irritation, but turned to the younger lady instead. 'Good morning, Victoria. I trust I see you both well?'

'As well as I ever am,' answered his mother in failing accents.

'And *I* would be a good deal better if I could only get to the place that I need to go to,' said Miss Victoria Mirfield in a meaningful tone.

'Where is it you need to go?' Jason asked, carefully lowering himself into a chair near his parent. Nobody would have supposed that they were related, let alone mother and son. She was fair, whereas he was dark, and her features were delicate, whilst his were strongly marked, even harsh. Only in implacable determination were they alike, but whereas the son was forthright, even domineering at times, the mother was quietly tenacious.

'I need to be at the modiste's,' Victoria replied. 'I have an . . . an extra fitting.' She coloured a little.

'An extra fitting,' Ballantyne repeated. 'And what would this be for?'

'For a gown,' Victoria replied defensively.

'But you do not need any extra fittings,' put in Mrs Ballantyne. 'Everything has been attended to.'

'There you are, you see,' said Ballantyne in

reasonable tones. 'You do not need to go after all. How fortunate!'

'I *do* need to go,' protested Miss Mirfield, almost stamping her foot. 'And what's more, I had arranged with Hattie — ' She broke off.

'Ah,' exclaimed the gentleman. 'So you are meeting Miss Harriet Yardy, not going to the modiste's.'

'Not at all,' replied Victoria quickly. 'Hattie needs an extra fitting so we thought . . . ' Her voice tailed off.

'Now let me make sure that I have this correctly,' said the colonel, longing to get to his feet but knowing that to maintain the fiction which he and Pitt had invented between them he ought to stay in his chair. 'You do not in fact have a fitting; it is Miss Yardy who has the fitting and you are meeting her there. This would not have anything to do with her brother, the handsome but feckless Captain Yardy, would it?'

'Hattie's brother does not visit modistes,' Victoria retorted indignantly.

'Just as well, then, that he has his little sister to collect notes for him,' said Ballantyne swiftly.

'Oh, Victoria,' uttered Mrs Ballantyne in failing accents. 'You have not been passing notes to men!' She uttered the last word with a strong note of revulsion in her voice.

'No, I have not!' declared Victoria indignantly. 'I would scorn to use such subterfuge. Besides,' she added naively, 'I don't like him very much any more.'

Jason gave a shout of laughter. 'Indeed, little cousin?' he exclaimed. 'And what has he done to earn your disdain?'

'I sat next to him at dinner and he makes stupid noises as he eats soup,' said Victoria candidly.

Jason laughed again, but Mrs Ballantyne agreed, nodding. 'That is quite a consideration. A man who has developed those kinds of habits will never change.' She looked fondly at her son. 'Jason now, eats his soup like a perfect gentleman. It is a pleasure to watch him.'

'Good God, Mama, never say that you sit and watch me eat soup,' protested her horrified son.

'Not now, of course,' answered his mother. 'But when you were little, I did so, and I must say that it has paid off wonderfully well.' She took a deep breath. 'As far as beer is concerned, however . . . '

The colonel struggled to his feet. 'Spare me, Mother,' he said hurriedly. 'Victoria, my dear, I am suddenly conscious of an overwhelming desire to accompany you to the modiste's.' Checking her delighted exclamation with an upraised hand, he went on, 'but only if we may go to Hatchard's on the way. I need to collect a book that they have procured for me.'

'Of course,' Victoria replied demurely.

'Oh, by the way, this was delivered for you just before I came in,' he added, handing her the note.

'Really, I think I ought to see it first,' complained Mrs Ballantyne. 'When I was a girl, we were never allowed to have any correspondence that our parents or guardians had not seen first.'

'Aunt Sophie!' protested Victoria.

'It may be from that Captain Yarbury, or whatever his name was.'

'It isn't even in his hand,' Victoria replied, then blushed hotly.

'Oho, so you know what that looks like, do you?' said Jason swiftly.

'Yes I do, and what's more I know what *your* hand looks like, and I have never had notes from you!'

'You do not need to tell *me* that,' put in Mrs Ballantyne. 'He is just like his dear papa. Not a single love letter did I get from him in all our years of courtship and marriage.'

'Well anyone is welcome to read this note,' said Victoria, having just made herself mistress of its contents. 'It is a letter reminding me to return my library books.'

'No doubt you will want me to take you to return those as well,' observed the colonel. 'Let us go, then.'

'Send Cray to fetch a hackney,' said Mrs Ballantyne. 'You must not walk all the way to Hatchard's.'

Ballantyne opened his mouth to object, then closed it again. His mother would never be able to keep his secret. He could not afford to give himself away to her, of all people.

'You really should not escort me to places, Jason,' said Miss Mirfield, as they entered the hackney, Ballantyne submitting to Cray's assistance with gritted teeth. The sympathetic butler, who had known the colonel all his life, supposed that Master Jason's leg must be paining him. 'It does get Aunt Sophie's hopes up so.'

'I'm afraid that having been appointed by your father to be your legal guardian, I have very little choice in the matter,' the colonel replied calmly.

'I must say, I wish that you could convince *her* of that,' said Victoria frankly. 'She will keep making plans, and I do hope that you are not terribly dashed, but I am afraid that they are plans destined never to come to fruition. You see' — she took a deep breath — 'although my friends all seem to be *aux*

134

anges over you, I am afraid I don't find you attractive *at all*.'

The colonel gave a shout of laughter. 'You cannot think how relieved I am to hear you say so,' he told her, as soon as he was able. 'For in my turn, I have to confess that your undoubted charms have no effect upon me whatsoever.'

'Oh,' said Miss Mirfield, not sure whether to be relieved or offended. Then, deciding that the matter was of no moment, she changed the subject, saying, 'As it happens, I have a reason of my own, now, for going to Hatchard's.'

He glanced across at her, his eyes narrowing. 'Lost your library books?' he asked.

'Certainly not,' Victoria retorted indignantly. 'At least,' she amended, 'not all of them. In fact, I have not lost any of them. I know exactly where they are.'

'Well?' he prompted.

'The . . . the history book is in my room,' she said carefully, thinking of the rather shocking novel hidden amongst her underwear in one of her drawers. 'The book of poetry will be rather more difficult to get hold of.'

'Where is it?'

'I think it may be on the way to China,'

Victoria confessed.

Another laugh. 'With Mrs Mannington, I suppose,' Ballantyne surmised, naming a friend of Victoria's whose husband had recently been appointed military attaché to an important diplomatic mission.

'Why yes,' Victoria agreed. 'So you see, I have to go to Hatchard's to buy a replacement.'

'It's to be hoped that the Chinese do not take offence at your friend's reading matter.'

'I do not see why they should,' responded Victoria, tossing her head. 'It is only a volume of poems by Mr Southey, and therefore quite unexceptionable.'

'Unlike the novel tucked away in one of your drawers, no doubt,' he observed.

'How did you know?' she exclaimed. 'Not that you are right, of course.'

'Of course not,' he replied, grinning. 'Never having been young myself, I naturally have no comprehension of such matters. In any case, I do not understand why you have to buy another copy of the book. Could you not simply take the money and let the shopkeeper buy another for himself?'

'I suppose I could,' Victoria agreed. 'If there is not a copy on the shelves, then that is what I shall do. To be completely honest with you, I thought I would get away with it. The owner of the business died, you see. But the note that came today tells me that there is a new proprietor.'

'So therefore, you are obliged to be honest.'

'Exactly so.'

'Where is this library, anyway?' he asked curiously, and with a feeling inside that was partly foreboding, partly excitement.

'In Clerkenwell, on the Green,' Victoria replied, as they arrived outside Hatchard's. She was too busy making sure that she descended from the carriage elegantly to notice the satisfied expression on her guardian's face. Yet another connection with Mrs Scorer, he thought. Fate was favouring him indeed.

★   ★   ★

Hatchard's very kindly provided benches outside for servants who were waiting for their employers, but Goodman was not yet there, so Eve went inside to a have a look around. The first thing that she noticed was that there were newspapers arranged on a table by the fireplace. Several people were making use of this facility by turning the pages of various periodicals that were on offer. Eve took out a notebook and pencil and sitting down on a chair that was a little out of the way, she made a note of this practice, together with the names of some of the papers that were on display. *The Morning Chronicle*, she wrote. *The London Gazette, The Morning Post, The Times.*

The papers did look very well thumbed, and there were two gentlemen leafing through the pages whilst another looked on, making comments. Did the shop really acquire the papers every day, or were they simply replaced occasionally? She would have to look more closely to see whether the daily papers actually were that day's.

What of the shop itself? It was clearly very well stocked and seemed to attract customers of all ages. Unobtrusively, she tried to count how many people were present, and of what age and sex they were.

Not wishing to draw attention to herself, she examined some of the books that were available, and finally decided to purchase a copy of Mary Wollstonecraft's *A Historical and Moral View of the French Revolution.* She had read Miss Wollstonecraft's *A Vindication of the Rights of Woman,* and thought her ideas interesting, but this work, though eight years old, had not come her way before. She also picked up *Clermont* by Regina Maria Roche. It looked like a gothic novel of the silliest variety, but it would be something to read in an idle moment.

It was only when she was walking towards the counter in order to pay for her purchases that it occurred to her that if she wanted something to read in her leisure time, she hardly needed to buy anything for she had a whole library and bookshop at her disposal. She almost laughed out loud and, as she looked up, her eyes alight with mirth, her gaze locked with that of a gentleman who was standing beside the table on which the newspapers lay. She did not recognize him immediately, but as he laid down the paper at which he had been looking, she realized to her dismay that he was one of the gentlemen who had been discourteous in Russell's coffee house.

He glanced around briefly, as if half expecting that her bright smile was directed at someone just behind him. Then, finding that this was not the case and clearly supposing, therefore, that she had smiled at him, he came forward, bowing politely.

'I realize that our previous encounter won't encourage you to acknowledge my acquaintance,' he said, 'but you smiled at me so sweetly just now that I'm hopeful that I'm forgiven. Max Hadleigh at your service.'

'Good day,' Eve replied, not wanting to speak to him at all, but seeing no alternative under the present circumstances save that of cutting him, a course of action that she was reluctant to pursue because it might draw attention to them. How she wished that he had not chosen to visit Hatchard's at that time, or, at the very least, that he had not looked at her as she had smiled!

'Might I be permitted to know the name of the lady I am addressing?' he asked. 'Or am I not forgiven after all?' His features were sharp, as Eve had noticed before, but he had a clever face and a mobile mouth.

'I am Mrs Scorer,' she replied. 'Shall we consider the matter forgotten?'

'You're too generous, ma'am,' he said, with another slight bow. 'Is Mr Scorer with you, perhaps?' He looked around the shop.

'I am a widow, sir,' Eve replied in uncompromising tones, wishing that she were decked out in black instead of in a gown of half-mourning which had simply seemed pretty when she had put it on but which now felt unforgivably frivolous given her station.

'I am sorry to hear that,' said Mr Hadleigh, sounding anything but. 'Have you come to live in London, or are you merely visiting?' His admiring glance took in her new outfit, and seemed to assess her figure as well.

'My plans are uncertain,' Eve replied. 'If you will excuse me, sir?' Yet again he inclined his head, and she walked past him to look at the newspapers. Now that she was closer to them, she could see that they were all daily periodicals and that they were up to date.

She had not realized that Hadleigh was still watching her, for she had carefully avoided looking at him. Now, he approached her once more and caught hold of her hand, just as she was putting it out to turn over the pages of one of the papers.

'Oh no, no,' he exclaimed in gentle tones of admonition. 'You will get that pretty glove quite soiled from handling newsprint.' Fixing her eyes with his, he slowly peeled her pale-grey glove off her right hand, making the action sensual in the extreme. Having done so, he laid it across his right wrist and solemnly presented it to her.

'Thank you,' she said shortly, trying not to blush as she took it from him. As she did so, the sound of the shop door closing caught her attention, and she looked across to see the arrogant gentleman whom she had seen in Berkeley Square that morning, and who had rescued her from Mr Hadleigh's advances in Russell's. He was accompanied by a statuesque young woman who looked to be in her late teens. This lady was dressed in the height of fashion, and her face, surrounded by golden ringlets and crowned by a charming straw bonnet, looked the picture of mischief. The gentleman looked at her, then at Hadleigh. His expression was disapproving. Eve reflected that he might look thus at a cat that he had rescued from the high branches of a tree, only to discover five minutes later that it was up the tree again.

Following her gaze, Hadleigh gave a start of surprise and stepped away from her to greet the newcomers. 'Miss Mirfield,' he murmured. 'Ballantyne.'

'Hadleigh,' the arrogant gentleman responded, his voice cold. Eve glanced up at him in surprise. It was the first time that she had heard his name mentioned. This gentleman, or someone related to him, must have been Edmund's commanding officer. She remembered that when she had first encountered him, he had been in uniform.

Miss Mirfield did not seem to be disturbed by her escort's lack of enthusiasm for the company in which he found himself. 'Mr Hadleigh,' she exclaimed. 'Fancy meeting you in Hatchard's! Have you come to purchase a book, or just to read the papers?'

He smiled impishly. 'I came in hopes of meeting you, ma'am. Can you doubt it?'

'Completely,' the young lady replied. 'You were very lucky after all. This is the first time I have come into Hatchard's for a fortnight.'

'Very lucky,' agreed Ballantyne, 'and not very gallant either. You are neglecting your companion, Hadleigh.'

Eve waited for the other man to say that they had met by chance. Instead, he smiled and said, 'How shameful that would be when I am the fortunate one rather than you today. But come, we must introduce the ladies. Or have you already met?'

As soon as she had heard the young lady referred to as Miss Mirfield, Eve knew that this moment would come. Taking the bull by the horns, she said, 'No, we have not met, although I feel as if I know Miss Mirfield already. I am Eve Scorer, and I handed a note to your butler just this morning.'

As she spoke, Eve saw the other lady's face flush a little, and some of the sparkle leave her eyes. Suddenly she realized, as she had not done before, that it must seem as if she, a tradeswoman — for so she must now consider herself — was expecting to bandy words with the ton. Consequently she herself began to blush.

It was Colonel Ballantyne who stepped into the breach. Eve had not observed his reaction to her name, but as she looked up at him now — and she did have to look quite a long way up for he was at least a foot taller than herself — she could see that he was smiling. 'If my cousin seems embarrassed, Mrs Scorer, it is because your letter reminded her that she has lost one of your books. You can easily imagine, therefore, what errand has brought us to Hatchard's.'

Eve was conscious of an overwhelming feeling of relief that she was not being snubbed, and she smiled back at him. 'Please, there is no need to purchase another book, Miss Mirfield,' she assured the other woman. 'I may even be able to replace it from my stock. Pray tell me, was it the poetry book that you mislaid or the — ?'

Miss Mirfield interrupted her, 'Or the improving history book?' she finished brightly.

'Or the improving history book, as you say,' Eve agreed smoothly.

'Or even the novel,' murmured the colonel.

'It is the poetry book,' Victoria replied, casting the colonel a look of outraged virtue.

'Then I am almost sure that there is another copy in the shop,' said Eve.

'You are a *shopkeeper*,' exclaimed Mr Hadleigh raising his brows. His tone was that of a man who, having thought that the item that he wanted was out of stock, now discovered that it was available after all. 'How very intriguing! Mrs Scorer, you grow more fascinating every time I meet you.'

His gaze was openly admiring, a thing that

144

Eve was not at all used to. If this was unnerving, even shocking, it was nothing compared to the astonishment that she felt when the colonel spoke.

'You may well believe it to be true, Hadleigh,' he declared, giving the impression that he knew Eve far better than was really the case.

'You have only met me twice,' she said rather tartly, looking at Hadleigh but referring to both of them. 'I doubt if the process will continue.'

'I'm sure it will,' answered Hadleigh. 'Like the first owner of your given name, I suspect that you will prove to be a constant source of temptation.'

'In that case, I will remove myself from your vicinity,' Eve replied crisply. 'Miss Mirfield, Mr Hadleigh, Colonel Ballantyne.'

It was the colonel who moved to hold the door open for her, but before she could step outside, he said, 'Mrs Scorer, I was your late husband's commanding officer.'

'I had suspected as much, sir,' Eve replied. 'Edmund often wrote about you in his letters. It is an honour to meet you.' The embarrassment of their previous encounter was temporarily forgotten, as at that moment she only remembered the sympathetic tone of his letter and the accounts that she had heard of his courage. She looked up into his face, her eyes glowing with admiration.

He inclined his head. 'He also told me about you,' he answered. 'I have his effects in my possession, and would be glad if you would tell me when I may wait upon you in order to return them, as is my duty.'

His words were all that was proper, but there was a coldness in his tone that Eve found a little unsettling, and it made her hesitate as she spoke. 'I . . . I am usually at home,' she murmured. 'If anyone is with me — '

'Surely any of your admirers would be willing to allow you five minutes to honour your husband's memory,' he interrupted.

She looked at him in some confusion, but before she could ask for an explanation he spoke again. 'I will call in a day or two, then.' Confusion about what he had said, made her hesitate in the doorway, and turn to look at him. Again he forestalled her. 'Pray satisfy my curiosity, ma'am,' he said. 'If you have your own bookshop to attend to, what are you doing here in Hatchard's?'

She could not resist. Looking straight up at him, she said in a confidential tone, 'I'm spying, Colonel.'

It was only when she was on her way home

in the hackney, having picked up Goodman from outside the shop, that she realized she had forgotten to buy the books she had selected.

11

'She seems very agreeable,' Victoria remarked after Eve had left the bookshop. Max Hadleigh had also left, bowing politely, and expressing the hope that they would meet soon. 'She's pretty, too. Did you not think so?'

The colonel grunted. Truth to tell, he had been very struck by Mrs Scorer. Her miniature had remained amongst his own things, and he had continued to look at it on a regular basis. Now, he was forced to admit that although it was a good likeness, it did not do her justice. The artist had caught the fine features, the pretty light-brown shade of her hair, and her sherry-coloured eyes. He had not been able to convey the animation of her features or the intelligence in her expression. It was a head and shoulders portrait, so naturally he had not been able to show the grace of her slim figure, so well set off by her elegantly cut gown.

What was he to make of her? On the one hand he had Captain Scorer's glowing opinion of her, an opinion surely coloured by distance; on the other, he had the evidence of his own eyes, which seemed to reveal a woman who was rather careless of her reputation. After all, he had just recently witnessed her enjoying a flirtatious encounter with a man whom he had warned off very recently. There was also the unfavourable account of her given by Julia Comberton. He knew that he had been inclined to idealize her almost as much as her husband had done, now he must be cautious for the sake of his mission.

Thoughts of this mission reminded him of that little remark that she had made as she had left Hatchard's. 'I'm spying, Colonel', she had said. What could she have meant?

On impulse, he said to Victoria, 'Come, we'll go on a visit. I want you to meet some new acquaintances of mine. Have you time before you are due to meet Miss Yardy at the modiste's?'

'I think so,' answered Victoria willingly. 'Anything to be seen with a war hero.'

'Baggage!' responded the colonel as they got into the carriage.

The journey from Hatchard's, Piccadilly to Brook Street was only a little further than their journey home, and the press of traffic not being very great, they were at the Combertons' house very quickly. Jason was glad that he had Victoria to talk to. It took his mind off the fact that he would far rather have been striding there on his own feet.

Truth to tell, he had had very little to do with Victoria since she had grown up, and was interested to see what kind of young woman she had become. His uncle, Francis Mirfield had, like himself, been a soldier, and had been killed in action when his daughter was only five. Mrs Mirfield, who before her marriage had been a Miss Ballantyne, had died when Victoria was thirteen, whereupon Jason's mother, who had been appointed co-guardian along with Jason himself, had packed her off to school in Islington, where she had remained until she was eighteen, just a year ago.

Major Mirfield had not been a wealthy man, and had never acquired an estate, but Victoria was his only child, and she would be the mistress of about £7000 on her majority, or on her marriage, if such marriage was with Jason's approval. She was not wealthy enough, therefore, to attract the greediest of fortune hunters; nevertheless, there would still be those who would respond to the alluring combination of a tidy sum of money, a pretty girl, and some distinguished society connections.

With this in mind, Jason decided to try and find out how up to snuff his cousin and ward was. 'What do you think to Max Hadleigh?' he asked her.

She frowned. 'He's quite handsome, although rather soft-looking, don't you think?'

Ballantyne grinned. 'You come from a family of soldiers, remember. Not everyone is or should be cast in that mould.'

'No, of course not. What I meant was that I simply do not like it when every second phrase is turned into a caress. I suspect he would say almost anything if he thought it would gain him an advantage.'

He laughed then. 'I am sure you are right. I must confess I am relieved.'

'Why?'

'Because I do not need to warn you away from him.'

'Oh no. But perhaps you need to perform that service for Mrs Scorer.'

His expression grew grim. 'I am sure that Mrs Scorer is well aware of what kind of man Hadleigh is,' he answered, thinking about how he had seen her in the man's company in Russell's. 'She is old enough to look after herself.'

'And besides, she will have Mr Scorer to look to her interests, I assume.'

'Mrs Scorer is a widow,' he said quickly.

'Oh? How do you know that?'

'Her husband was one of my officers. A fine one too; I was grieved to lose him.'

'Then perhaps you ought to warn her. Poor soul! She is surely in some measure your responsibility.'

He opened his mouth to tell her to hold her tongue, then reflected that this was hardly fair, when he had been thinking exactly the same thing.

At this point, they arrived in Brook Street, and were soon being shown into the drawing room where Mrs Comberton was entertaining a visitor. 'I do not suppose you have met Mr Bunty before,' she said, as she introduced them. 'He is a neighbour of ours, and almost like a member of the family.'

'Your first visit to London, sir?' Ballantyne asked him, as they exchanged courtesies. He recalled that Mrs Comberton had said that this was the man with whom Mrs Scorer had been flirting, even while she was still in mourning.

Bunty shook his head. 'I have been before, but not very recently. I am kept quite busy at home, looking after the estate.'

'Do you farm your estate alone, Mr Bunty?' Victoria asked him. His appearance impressed her. He was tall and well built, with blond hair, and there was about him none of the softness which she had found so unappealing in Max Hadleigh.

'No, I help my father and my brother

Jeremy,' he answered. 'The estate is a sizeable one, so it keeps us all busy. But since Mrs Comberton needed an escort to come to London, I decided to make a visit of my own.'

'Is it not kind of him?' said Julia. 'Colonel, are you quite comfortable on that sofa? It is not too low?'

'It is very comfortable, thank you, ma'am,' Ballantyne replied.

'Horace, pour some wine for Miss Mirfield and the colonel,' said Mrs Comberton. 'How is your mother, Colonel? Is she well?'

As Jason was answering his hostess's enquiry, he noted that after bringing the two visitors a glass, Bunty sat down next to Victoria and engaged her in conversation. After a moment or two's observation, he concluded that his ward was quite happy in the man's company, and gave his attention to his hostess, who had taken her place next to him on the sofa.

'Such a charming man,' she said, dropping her voice a little. 'I have met a number of charming men in my time, Colonel Ballantyne.' She looked up at him from under her lashes.

'Indeed, ma'am?' he replied.

'I do hope you are not one of them,' she went on.

'I'll do my best not to be,' he answered

bluntly, not sure where this conversation might be leading.

She laughed gently. 'Somehow with charming men, one feels that there is no substance, and I do so like a man to be . . . substantial.' Her hand fluttered a little, brushing against his thigh so lightly that it might almost have been accidental, had he not seen the look in her eye.

At once, he could feel his hackles rising. Ever since his officer's wife had attempted to seduce him all those years ago, he had had a deep distrust of predatory females. He could play his part in gentle, light-hearted flirtation, although he never felt at his most comfortable in such situations. He also enjoyed more basic encounters with ladies of a certain kind; this kind of encounter though was not at all to his liking.

Thankfully for his peace of mind, at this moment some other visitors arrived, Julia got up to greet them, and the conversation became more general, until it was time for Jason and Victoria to leave. Once they were in the carriage, Victoria said, 'Well that is a disappointment, I must say.'

'A disappointment? What do you mean?'

'A disappointment for you,' she replied. 'I had quite thought that Mrs Scorer would suit you very nicely, but it turns out that she is as good as promised to Mr Bunty.'

'Did he say so?' Jason asked, glad to have something to take his mind off Mrs Comberton.

'Apparently he was paying court to her when she left for London without even bidding leave of him. He has come to Town to discover in what way he might have offended her. He asked my help, actually.'

'I hope you said no,' said Jason quickly, alarmed, although he would have been hard put to it to say why.

'Well I did, since I did not feel that I knew either of them well enough to be of any use. But it has occurred to me that if Mr Bunty is successful in his errand, then he will be able to protect her from Max Hadleigh, and others like him.'

'So he will,' answered Jason, reflecting on the fact that there was a subtle difference between Julia's account of Eve's dealings with Bunty, and Bunty's own version of their relationship. Could Eve really be so capricious that neither Julia nor Bunty knew what she really wanted?

He now discovered with surprise that he must have a perverse streak in his nature of which he had previously been unaware. Everything that he had learned about Mrs Scorer so far had been prompting him towards the conclusion that he should not have anything to do with her. Yet when it seemed likely that another man, for example Mr Bunty, might be in a position to protect her, he found himself very reluctant to entrust the task to anyone else.

12

The following day, a letter arrived for Miss Sparrow from her father, the general. 'How odd,' said that lady as she opened it at the breakfast-table. 'In some ways, it seems ages since I was at home; and yet there has been so much to do that in other respects it seems as though time has gone by in a flash.'

'Yes, it is odd,' Eve answered. 'Is the general well, Lavinia?'

'He appears to be,' Miss Sparrow replied. 'He is a little concerned about the corresponding societies.'

'I thought that they had had their day,' Eve remarked, all unconsciously echoing Colonel Ballantyne's words to Mr Pitt on another occasion.

'Yes, I believe that Mr Pitt put a stop to all that,' Miss Sparrow agreed. 'By the way, have you decided what to do about that young Frenchman?'

'Not yet,' Eve replied. 'Goodman thinks that I ought to give him a trial. I am to see him today, and I will try to conduct some sort of interview to find out his capabilities. Though what I am to ask him, I cannot imagine.'

'You could ask him how he thinks a bookshop should be run,' Miss Sparrow suggested.

'An excellent thought! If I do not employ him, I will at least be able to steal his ideas!'

The young Frenchman was already waiting outside when Goodman unbolted the door. Eve had decided that she would conduct her interview in the back room, where they would be less likely to be interrupted. He came in rather diffidently as before and, as he took the chair that Eve indicated, she noticed that his linen, though clean and of good quality, looked rather old and that his cuffs were worn.

With Miss Sparrow's advice in mind, she asked her first question. 'You told me yesterday, *monsieur*, that you had worked for Mme Lascelles in this shop. You must have some grasp of what the business involves. Would you be so good as to tell me what you think are the main features of it?'

M. D'Angers spoke shyly at first, but when he realized that Eve was genuinely interested and not simply trying to trap him, he gained confidence, and soon revealed that he had a very good grasp of what went on in the establishment.

'Not many Frenchmen would choose to be in London at this time,' Eve said eventually.

'Why do you remain here? You must know that Napoleon has signed an amnesty allowing you to return.'

He shook his head. 'I cannot,' he replied. 'The amnesty does not apply to all *émigré* families. My father was too fiercely supportive of the Bourbons for his attitude to be overlooked by the Corsican. I should not be permitted to return. Besides, there is nothing left there for me.'

He did not elaborate on this remark and Eve, not wanting to bring to his mind memories that might be painful for him, changed the subject. 'I went to Hatchard's yesterday and had a good look round, and I have come back with some ideas which I would like to share with you. Perhaps you would tell me what you think?' She told him about the table with the newspapers on display and he listened with interest. 'I was wondering whether we might do something of that nature. What do you think?'

The young man nodded. 'I have heard of this, and I think it would be very popular,' he said. 'A fire could be lit when the weather becomes colder, and perhaps there might be some more comfortable chairs to encourage people to linger.'

'That is a good idea,' Eve agreed. 'Something I did notice, however, was that there were no publications specifically for ladies. Do you think that we might have more than one table, with one set aside for periodicals such as *The Ladies' Monthly Museum?*'

At this moment, the doorbell rang, but Eve, hearing Goodman going to the door, remained where she was.

M. D'Angers nodded in response to her last remark. 'You could have several tables set out as if it were a coffee house,' he suggested.

'We could even serve coffee,' agreed Eve. 'M. D'Angers, I have made a decision: you're hired.'

The young man beamed, and seized hold of both her hands. '*Merci, madame!*' he exclaimed. '*Merci mille fois!*' He then proceeded to kiss both her hands, one after the other. It was singularly unfortunate that Goodman ushered Colonel Ballantyne into the room just as he was doing this.

'Colonel Ballantyne!' exclaimed Eve, snatching her hands away from the Frenchman. Suddenly she recalled the colonel's remark concerning her admirers.

'Mrs Scorer,' responded the colonel, bowing. 'I hope I am not intruding.'

'Not at all,' Eve replied, her colour heightened, much to her annoyance. 'I have just informed M. D'Angers that I am willing

to employ him in my shop and he was
. . . was expressing his gratitude. I do not
know whether you have met M. D'Angers,
Colonel? M. D'Angers, this is Colonel
Ballantyne.'

As the two men exchanged courtesies, Eve
had leisure to consider how odd it was that
she should be introducing the colonel to
someone when in fact she had never been
formally introduced to the man.

'D'Angers,' the colonel was saying thoughtfully. 'You would be a connection of the
Marquis de Varenne, I suppose?'

'His cousin, *m'sieur*,' answered D'Angers
politely. 'But I am now the last of my line.'

'I'm sorry to hear it.' Ballantyne turned to
Eve. 'You will forgive me if I sit down? I find
that I cannot stand for long these days.'

'Yes, of course,' Eve replied. 'Perhaps you
would like to come upstairs to my sitting-
room. Or would you rather not negotiate the
stairs?'

The colonel raised his brows at her
suggestion, and she blushed, suddenly feeling
that she had suggested something scandalous.
'I would prefer not to have to do so,' he
answered frankly.

'Then please be seated, and I will desire
Goodman to bring some wine for us all.' She
rang the bell.

'Not for me, thank you,' said D'Angers. 'I am expected elsewhere, but I will bid you good day, Colonel, and you, too, *madame*, with many, many thanks once more for your kindness.'

After he had gone, Eve turned to the colonel. He was sitting in one of the six upright chairs that were placed around a polished, serviceable looking table, set in the middle of the room. Before sitting down, he had turned his chair so that it was slightly sideways on to the table, and he now sat with his left hand leaning on top of the table, his right resting lightly on his thigh. Even in civilian clothes, there was something military-looking about him.

'I think you must be aware of the purpose of my visit,' he said, bending to pick up a bundle which he had brought with him and which he had laid on the floor beside his chair.

'Let me help you,' said Eve, thinking of his knee. She crouched down to assist him and, as she did so, their hands touched. He drew in his breath with a hiss, she looked up at him, met his gaze, and suddenly realized one reason why he might have been nicknamed Colonel Blazes.

'Let be, madam,' he said through his teeth. 'I can manage.'

'I beg your pardon,' she said. 'I only sought to help you.'

'Help from women of your doubtful reputation is something I can well do without,' he retorted.

She straightened, wondering if she could possibly have heard him correctly. She was still staring at him when Goodman came in with the wine.

'It's good to see you, Goodman, and under rather different circumstances,' said the colonel.

'It is that, sir,' Goodman agreed, coming to attention as soon as he had set his tray down on the table. 'That was a bad business, losing the general,' he added, referring to General Sir Ralph Abercrombie, who had perished during the Egyptian campaign. He poured out two glasses of wine and gave them to the colonel and to Eve.

'It was indeed,' Ballantyne agreed gravely. He turned to Eve. 'If you have Goodman working for you then you're very fortunate,' he said. 'He was a first-rate sergeant, and as cool a man under fire as any I've seen.'

'Saving yourself, sir,' Goodman put in. 'How is your leg healing?'

'I'm told that I can't hope for it to improve much now,' Ballantyne replied. 'I've got to live with it as it is.'

'I'm sorry to hear that, sir,' commented Goodman, before bowing and withdrawing.

Once they were alone again, Eve drew a deep breath and put her glass down. 'Now, sir, you will explain, if you please, the outrageous remark that you made to me just before Goodman came in.'

'I am simply here to return Captain Scorer's belongings to you,' Ballantyne replied, rather tight-lipped. 'I prefer to say no more on the subject.'

'I am sure you do,' Eve answered contemptuously. 'I must insist, however, that you give some explanation for your outrageous rudeness.'

'You insist, do you? Very well then, I will give it to you. I'm a soldier, ma'am, and my officers are like my family. Their feelings, their safety, their reputations are all of great importance to me. Captain Scorer was a fine officer and a brave man. With his dying breath, he commended you to my care.'

At mention of Edmund, Eve's face softened. 'His dying breath? You were with him when he died?'

'He died in my arms,' the colonel replied bleakly. 'I returned to England, determined to carry out his last wish. He spoke of you with such affection, such admiration — ' He broke off. 'I thank God that he never discovered, as

164

I have done, that his loyalty was misplaced.'

'What do you mean, you have *discovered*? In what does this disloyalty consist? Upon my word, sir, you must answer me. I have a right to know.'

'I have observed your fast behaviour with my very own eyes, madam.'

'My fast behaviour? What on earth can you mean?'

'Oh come, madam! Did you not sit in Russell's alone, then permit a man whom you had never met before to put you into a hackney, even inviting him to join you in it? Did you not behave scandalously towards Max Hadleigh, a notorious womanizer if ever there was one, encouraging him to flirt with you and permitting him to peel off items of your clothing in a public place? Did you not today receive a young Frenchman alone and allow him to cover your hands with kisses? Are you not receiving me alone even now?'

She listened to this speech with gathering wrath. 'You have no right to criticize me for any of those incidents,' she declared, exasperated. 'I cannot possibly be blamed for being in Russell's, for example.'

'Did someone else put you in there?' Ballantyne asked her, his brows soaring.

'No, but I had a perfect right to be there,' she retorted spiritedly. 'How was I to know that boxing-mad men would overrun the place?'

'Possibly by paying heed to Russell's warnings, and don't tell me that he didn't do so, for I shouldn't believe you.'

'That is beside the point,' she replied, annoyed because he was right in his supposition, and determined not to admit it. 'A lady should be able to purchase a cup of coffee without the risk of insult.'

'A lady would be able to do so if she patronized the right establishments.'

'A lady ought to be able to purchase a cup of coffee in *any* establishment,' she asserted.

'You are describing the world as you would like it to be rather than the world as it is,' he remarked.

'Perhaps. But, sir, to criticize me for offering you a seat in my carriage is most ungracious. How, pray, am I to treat a hero of the Egyptian campaign? By leaving him to limp through the streets?'

'You throw my disability in my face, ma'am,' he said, his face set.

'I did not intend to, but I will not pretend that it does not exist. Anyway, I do not see that it is right to castigate me for seeking to perform an act of mercy.'

'Very well, ma'am. I will concede that on that occasion you acted from the best of motives, however misguided. But you were not wise to allow such as Max Hadleigh to behave scandalously towards you.'

'He did not behave scandalously,' Eve protested; then she remembered the glove incident and blushed.

'Precisely, ma'am,' said the colonel ironically. 'And before you say that Miss Mirfield flirted with him, let me remind you that she was chaperoned by her cousin and guardian.'

'You are her guardian?' echoed Eve, momentarily diverted.

'I am, for my sins,' he retorted. 'However, it is not her behaviour that is under discussion, but yours.'

'I beg to differ,' Eve replied. '*You* may be trying to discuss it: *I* fail to see why it is any of your business.'

'You make it my business when you draw such attention to yourself that other people express their concern.'

'Other people? What other people?' Eve demanded.

'Your own cousin, ma'am, in whose house you have been residing until very recently,' he replied. 'Apparently your conduct towards her neighbours leaves something to be desired.'

'Good God, Horace Bunty,' she murmured, losing some of her colour. To the colonel, in his suspicious state of mind, it almost looked like an admission of guilt.

'Yes. Mr Bunty is the gentleman,' he responded. 'I suppose I should be thankful that you knew immediately to whom I was referring. It does at least suggest that you have confined your attentions to only one neighbour. You will be glad to know that he is in London, and is prepared to renew his suit. I am astonished to learn that he should wish to do so when you have clearly been playing fast and loose with him. I would strongly advise you to accept him, ma'am. You obviously need a husband to keep you in check.'

'You appear to be sadly misinformed,' she told him. 'Mr Bunty is not interested in marriage.'

'My God, then, ma'am, you are even more brazen than I thought,' he exclaimed.

She turned pale as she took in the meaning of his remark. 'How dare you?' she spat out. 'You know nothing about me. You have no right to criticize or to advise me.'

'I was your husband's commanding officer,' he began, 'and I — '

'Yes you were, but I have yet to learn that you are mine,' she interrupted. 'You have made a lot of judgements about things that you have seen me do. Perhaps some of them were not very wise, but I do not deserve your criticisms on the basis of those actions. You have also heard things about me, and many of the things you have heard are mistaken. Well, I have heard a great deal about you, too, mostly from my husband. In his letters he told me of your courage, your gallantry and your humanity. He idolized you, Colonel Ballantyne; and such were his tales of you that I almost came to regard you in the same light. He told me that in the event of his death, he would take comfort from the fact that you would look to my care. I have your letter — '

She broke off, as all the emotions that she had felt on receiving the letter came flooding back, and to her great chagrin, she felt a lump come to her throat, and a prickling at the back of her eyes. Determinedly, she dashed away the tears with her hand. 'I know it by heart,' she went on. 'It was the one thing that — ' She broke off again. 'Never mind that now. The one thing Edmund failed to reveal to me, sir, was your appalling lack of judgement. If you jump to erroneous conclusions so rapidly in the field, I am amazed that you survived five minutes, let alone that you have lived to become a colonel.'

'Mrs Scorer — ' he began.

Eve could not stand any more. She shut

her eyes, and made a dismissive gesture with her hands. 'Oh, why do you not just go away and . . . and harry the French, or something? You have annoyed me quite enough for one day.' She turned her back on him, leaning with both hands on the table, far too overwrought to say more. She heard him murmur her name again, then when she turned back, he was gone.

13

No sooner had Ballantyne left than the door to the kitchen opened and Mrs Castle came hurrying in. 'Oh, Mrs Scorer, please forgive me for interrupting you, but Mr Goodman said as how you had The Colonel here.' She pronounced the letters of his rank as if they were written in capital letters.

'Colonel Ballantyne has been here, if that is who you mean, Mrs Castle,' Eve replied her face averted. She was surprised that her voice was so steady.

'Never say that I have missed him,' replied the widow, her face falling.

'I fear you have,' Eve replied.

'Well, no doubt — ' Mrs Castle broke off. 'Why, Mrs Scorer, you're crying. Whatever can be the matter?' Eve could not think what to say. Fortunately, Mrs Castle saw the bundle with Edmund's belongings inside, together with his sword, and drew her own conclusions. 'Oh, Mrs Scorer, did he bring your husband's things? I'm sorry, ma'am, really I am.'

Eve did not correct her. Somehow, she did not think that the cook would understand.

Truth to tell, once she had started crying she was finding it hard to stop. It was not that she had not shed tears over Edmund's death — she had. It was, perhaps, that at the time she had had her mother-in-law's grief to think of, and little Luke; then the death of Edmund's mother so soon afterwards had meant that she had had to get her own grieving over and done with rather more quickly than was really healthy. Mrs Castle, a motherly soul, put her arms around her and then when her sobs began to subside, found a huge clean handkerchief for her to dry her tears.

'There now, ma'am,' she said. 'Better out than in, that's what I always say. How about a nice cup of tea? Then you can tell me a bit about your husband, if you like. This wine is all very well for the gentlemen, but in my opinion it doesn't soothe like a cup of tea.'

Eve smiled weakly. 'Thank you, Mrs Castle. That would be very pleasant.'

After the cook had left the room, taking the tray with the glass as she went, Eve sat down to look at the contents of the bundle. Like Ballantyne, she found herself marvelling that a life should somehow have become distilled down to these few objects.

She picked up the signet ring. Edmund had never had big hands, and the ring which he had worn on the third finger of his left hand, fitted her middle finger nicely. She had a sudden recollection of Colonel Ballantyne's right hand as it had rested on his powerfully muscled thigh. This ring would probably not even fit onto his smallest finger. She would put it away for Luke to have when he was older. The watch, too, would be his, as would most of the rest of his father's possessions. The Prayer Book he could have very soon. It would encourage him with his reading.

As she looked at the collection of items, it came into her mind that something was missing, but she could not think what it could be. Perhaps some items had been lost or destroyed on the field of battle. Of one thing she could be quite certain: Colonel Ballantyne would not withhold anything that properly belonged to her or to her son. He would be far too high-minded for that.

She thought about the sweeping judgement that he had made about her and all her indignation came flooding back. 'How dare he?' she exclaimed. 'How dare he?' True, she had not been very wise in all her actions. For him to take the word of others, however, and make deductions about her was quite unforgivable. How could he believe her cousin's nonsense so easily? Would that Julia had not come to London. She had done her utmost to make her life a misery at Stonecrop Manor. It now seemed that she would do her best to spoil things in London too, by blackening Eve's character.

Thoughts of Julia made her recall the unwelcome news that Horace Bunty was in London. She could not doubt that he was in pursuit of her, and the very idea of it made her feel sick. When she was a penniless dependent, seduction had been his aim, never mind the consequences to her. Now, she was a woman of property, so perhaps he really was thinking of marriage, as Ballantyne had implied. If he supposed that she would give him a single glance, he was very much mistaken. At least she was no longer undefended. Goodman would protect her, as would Lavinia and Mrs Castle. Of the Todds she was less certain. They did their work well enough, but there was no real human contact with them. Sometimes Eve felt as if when she spoke to them she was almost using another language.

The man who could have protected her from Horace Bunty with one hand tied behind his back had just left. Because he held her in such low esteem, she would never lower herself to ask him. She was conscious of a deep sense of disappointment that the noble, compassionate man who had written to her should now be obscured by the pompous, disapproving man who chose to misjudge her on such slim evidence.

Her mind was brought back to the present by the clatter of the tea tray.

'There we are,' Mrs Castle said comfortably, as she set it down. 'If I'd thought, I'd have taken it up to your sitting room. Would you like me to do so, ma'am?'

Eve shook her head. 'No, thank you. I still look a little overwrought, I fear, and I don't want Luke to see me and perhaps be alarmed.'

'The poor colonel,' murmured Mrs Castle. 'He'll have been very sorry to be the cause of your distress, however unwittingly.'

Naturally not wanting to respond to this, Eve said instead, 'Did your husband serve under him for long, Mrs Castle?'

'Yes, he did, and thought the world of him, as did all the men. 'Blazes' they used to call him.'

'Yes, I know that nickname,' Eve replied. 'Where did it come from, I wonder?' She thought of the expression in his eyes.

'It's because he was first in and last out, no matter what his injuries.'

'Really?'

'There was one occasion when he saved my Billy's life. Billy was struck down and the

175

colonel stood over him and fought off the enemy until there was a pause in the fighting, and my man could be got to safety. And all that when the colonel was wounded himself, too, and fighting with his left hand, because his right was useless. There's some officers who wouldn't have bothered for a sergeant, but the colonel wasn't like that.'

'Was that in Egypt?' Eve asked.

Mrs Castle shook her head. 'No, in Ceylon.'

'Did you follow the drum?' Eve asked curiously.

'I did at first, miss, but later on Joanna became that nervy, I hadn't the heart to take her with me, and there was no one I could leave her with. After Billy had . . . had died, it was the colonel himself who came to see me. It almost broke my heart again to see him so badly injured. He said he'd make sure I was provided for, and without his help we'd have had nothing at all when you came to see us.'

'That was good of him,' Eve acknowledged.

'Oh he is, ma'am,' Mrs Castle assured her. 'He looked splendid in his red and gold. But then you would know that, Captain Scorer having served under him and all.'

Eve shook her head. 'I only met him a few days ago,' she confessed.

'You do surprise me,' replied Mrs Castle.

'He's not handsome of course, but he's what I'd call a real man. He got a few second looks from one or two ladies as I could mention, I can tell you! One or two of the other officers' wives used to cast their eyes his way. There was one I remember who was no better than she should be, that . . . but there, ma'am, I shouldn't be so gossipy in that sort of way, should I? Well, I'd best get back to the kitchen, otherwise there'll be no dinner.'

After Mrs Castle had gone, Eve sat at the table slowly unwrapping the things that the colonel had brought then smoothing and folding the canvas and rolling the string.

The cook's words had given her pause for thought. She could well imagine the heroic scene, with the badly wounded colonel standing firm over the body of the fallen soldier. It occurred to her that Goodman would also have stories to tell about his former commanding officer. She could also imagine how women would be drawn to him, with his fine physique . . .

'Except, of course, I do not have the slightest interest in him,' she told herself firmly. To take her mind off the unpleasant encounter with the colonel, she sat down to make further sense of the notes that she had made at Hatchard's and in no time was writing letters, ordering newspapers to be delivered to the shop.

* * *

As Colonel Ballantyne left the premises he caught sight of Todd sweeping the steps outside. 'Do you work for Mrs Scorer?' he asked curiously.

Todd paused briefly in his task, then carried on without responding. Ballantyne was about to speak to the man again, when Goodman appeared with a ladder.

'Just going to repaint the sign, Colonel,' said Goodman.

At that, Todd halted in his task and looked up. 'Colonel,' he said.

'That's right,' said Goodman with gentle approval. 'This is Colonel Blazes.'

'Colonel,' Todd said again, straightening, and holding his broom at his side, almost like a musket at rest.

Ballantyne smiled at him, said 'Carry on soldier,' then turned to Goodman. 'Look after your mistress. These are uncertain times.'

As the colonel travelled back to his house, it would have been hard to say whether he was more annoyed with Eve Scorer or with himself. He had jeopardized his mission by losing his temper with her, making it difficult for him to return to the bookshop. He, who managed to keep cool under murderous fire, had allowed himself to lose control over a woman!

Yet she, too, had lost control, storming at him, giving as good as she got. If nothing else, he had to admire her courage. Then she had started to cry and the doubts that had been at the back of his mind from the very beginning had come to the fore.

He hated seeing a woman cry. He had seen a number of them use tears as a means of getting attention, making play with a handkerchief, peeping over the top of it so as to arouse masculine sympathy. His mother was quite capable of such tricks. With a flash of insight, he concluded that Mrs Comberton would be another such. That kind of display left him unmoved. But when Eve Scorer had cried, she had tried to conceal it and to hold back the tears. She had turned her back upon him rather than let him see her distress, and she had shown no inclination to throw herself into his arms in order to claim some comfort.

What would she have done, he wondered, if he had embraced her and dried her tears with his handkerchief? How would she have reacted then?

This was such a disturbing reflection that he decided to think instead about how he could get himself back into her good graces. He had the perfect excuse to go again, for he could escort Victoria to the shop in order to return her library book. Then, once there, he could make his apologies for his rudeness. He could put it down to the pain that he was in on account of his wound. He shifted uncomfortably in his seat. He disliked this subterfuge that had been thrust upon him. It was quite contrary to his nature. He tried to comfort himself with the thought that the safety of the realm must be his first consideration here. Everything else must come second to that.

Undoubtedly the best way forward would be to get up a flirtation with Mrs Scorer, as Pitt had suggested. He could then make further contact with Goodman at the same time. He had made some headway in meeting D'Angers, and more visits to the shop would enable him to find out more about the young Frenchman as well. Part of his mind urged that this was unworthy, but he hastily repressed these thoughts. This was a matter of war, and war always had its casualties.

⋆ ⋆ ⋆

M. D'Angers began work the following day, and Eve soon found him plenty to do. She had made the decision to open the shop and library in a week's time, and in preparation for this, she gave him the task of making sure that this fact was set out in all the London papers. He was also entrusted with designing a single page advertisement to be handed to people locally as they travelled through Clerkenwell Green. There was a reliable printer working nearby who was willing to prepare such advertisements at a reasonable cost.

After D'Angers had gone, Eve sat down to write personal letters to all the people who normally patronized the library. There would be a grand opening of the shop in one week's time, with refreshments, she told them. She had not yet decided what refreshments would be served.

Goodman willingly took Eve's letters to a variety of addresses in London and, on one or two occasions, brought back the encouraging information that the recipients would be delighted to attend. Evidently the scandalous reputation that Colonel Ballantyne had predicted had not gone before her.

For a consideration, a couple of lads from the nearby inn were prepared to give out handbills, and eventually, Eve felt that she had done all that was humanly possible to ensure the success of her little venture.

She was carefully ticking items off a list in front of her when the doorbell rang, and she heard Goodman come through from the kitchen in order to see who was there. There was a sound of male voices, then Goodman came in to tell her that two gentlemen had come to visit her. She was not at all sure about how she felt with regard to entertaining male visitors unchaperoned. Then she reminded herself that she was a businesswoman and a widow, not a debutante in her first season. With her work about her, however, she would have plenty of excuse for telling them that they could not stay long, so she stood up ready to receive them.

'The Comte de Monceux and Mr Harpin,' Goodman announced.

'Good morning, gentlemen,' Eve said, recognizing the name of the second visitor. 'I am Mrs Scorer. I fear that this establishment is not yet open for business.'

'Mrs Scorer,' said the thinner of the two men. 'I am Percival Harpin at your service. I am aware that your business is not yet officially open. I have received your invitation to the grand opening next week and hope very much to attend.'

'I am pleased to hear that, Mr Harpin,' replied Eve. 'Goodman, would you please desire Miss Sparrow to come downstairs? Then you may bring refreshments for my guests.'

Once he had gone, Harpin said, 'You must allow me to introduce my friend the Comte de Monceux.'

'How do you do, *m'sieur*,' said Eve politely. 'Have you visited this establishment before?'

The *comte* bowed. Eve estimated that the men were both about forty years of age. Harpin was thin, wiry-looking, pale and somewhat nondescript in appearance, and Eve could imagine that the moment he left the shop, she would instantly forget what he looked like. This impression was increased by the fact that he was dressed almost entirely in dove grey. Monceux, on the other hand, was thickset, dark and good-looking in a fleshy, Mediterranean style, and was probably used to making many a female heart beat faster. He was dressed elegantly but perhaps a little more flamboyantly than was generally the custom.

'But no, *madame*,' the *comte* replied, in heavily accented English. 'I have spent little time in England.'

'I am showing my friend around our capital city,' Harpin put in. 'He is anxious to learn more about our country.'

'I hope that you like what you have seen so

far,' Eve said, inviting them to be seated with a gesture.

'Believe me, *madame*, I am enchanted by everything English,' replied the *comte* smiling at her and moistening his lips as he took his seat.

His manner left her a little flustered, so she was glad when Goodman returned.

'Miss Sparrow is not on the premises, ma'am,' he said. 'She has taken Master Luke for a walk.'

'Then please ask Mrs Castle to bring coffee and biscuits, and afterwards return and attend me here.'

After he had left the room, Harpin said 'I have a special reason for coming today, as I am sure you will guess. I am returning the book on plants of the tropics, which I had borrowed before the sad death of Mme Lascelles.'

'Thank you,' she replied, as he placed it on the table.

'Her loss must have been a great grief to you, *madame*,' said the *comte* politely.

'I hardly know how to answer you, sir,' Eve replied, after a moment's thought. 'The truth is that although I was distantly related to Mme Lascelles, I never met her. I grieve at her passing, as one must always grieve at a death, but my feelings of loss are not personal.'

'*M. le Comte* is hoping that you will be of

help to him, Mrs Scorer,' said Harpin.

'I will certainly help in any way I can,' Eve responded, thinking to herself, in any way that is proper.

'You are most kind,' Monceux acknowledged. 'I am very anxious to improve my English, and my friend M. Harpin has suggested that I take out a subscription, so that I may borrow books at my leisure.'

At this point Goodman returned to take up a position behind Eve's chair, but further back so that he did not intrude upon the proceedings.

'You are very welcome to do so, *m'sieur*,' Eve responded. She was very glad, now, that she had looked into the records of the shop and library and knew how the business was conducted. 'If, however, you do not intend to be in London for long, you might prefer to borrow books on a different basis, simply depositing the value of the book that you choose each time, from which I would deduct a small fee.'

Mrs Castle came in at this point with coffee and biscuits, and while she was setting the tray down, the *comte* said, 'I think that I would prefer to pay the subscription.'

'Then the charge to you would be sixteen shillings for the year, or five shillings for a quarter.'

'That seems very reasonable, for so much reading matter,' Monceux observed. 'Do you have many people who have not returned their books, or are they all law-abiding like my friend Harpin?'

They conversed pleasantly for a while over the coffee cups, but Eve could not feel at ease. The *comte* was too attentive, and altogether too fascinated with the work of a London bookseller. Furthermore, whilst the Frenchman was doing all the talking, Harpin sat impassively, listening and looking round. Of the two men, Eve was not sure which one unnerved her the most, and she was very glad of Goodman's reassuringly solid presence at her back.

They had just finished their coffee when the door opened and M. D'Angers walked in. Monceux was saying something to Eve, so whilst Harpin turned his head towards the newcomer, the *comte* remained with his back to the door. On hearing the *comte*'s voice, D'Angers stood for a moment or two as if frozen to the spot, before coming forward to acknowledge first his hostess, then Harpin, and finally saying, 'Monceux, it has been some time.'

The *comte* rose from his place bowing politely, but his rather oily smile not adorning his features for once. 'D'Angers. It has, as you

186

say, been a long time. How do you fare?'

'As well as any loyal king's subject far from home,' D'Angers responded, his chin raised belligerently. 'And yourself?'

'I am well,' the *comte* returned. Then he turned to Eve with a bow. '*Madame*, it has been a pleasure, but I believe we must not intrude upon your valuable time any longer.'

Harpin also rose. 'We look forward to seeing you again when this shop is formally opened,' he said.

'You will be very welcome, gentlemen,' Eve responded. To her surprise, it seemed as though M. D'Angers would forget his normally impeccable manners and fail to bid their guests farewell. '*M'sieur?*' she prompted him.

'Your servant, *messieurs*,' he said, bowing rather stiffly.

If Eve had intended to enquire into the reasons for her employee's rudeness she was to find that her enquiries would be unnecessary.

'Poltroon!' he spat at the closed door. 'Traitor!'

'I beg your pardon?' Eve asked him.

'Whilst gallant blood was spilled on the guillotine and brave men were seeking to help their king, others were licking the boots of those whom they perceived to be on their way to glory,' declared the Frenchman, his eyes flashing. 'Bonaparte appeaser! Estate snatcher! Pah! I spit upon him! Excuse me, *madame*. I must be alone for a time. I am too overset to speak.'

After he had gone, Eve turned to Goodman with a wry grin. 'To think that I thought that running a library would be a peaceful occupation,' she said.

★ ★ ★

'The question is, M. D'Angers, do we serve wine or coffee?' Eve said at last, everything else having been decided upon. 'I do not think that we have enough room or enough staff to serve both.'

'As it is the opening of your venture, perhaps wine would be more appropriate,' suggested the young Frenchman. After his dramatic exit, he had returned an hour later with an apology, and an expression on his face which discouraged questions. Eve decided not to try to extract further confidences. Perhaps the arrival of the two men for the grand opening would encourage D'Angers to say more about the subject.

'Yes, I think the same,' Eve agreed. 'But where do I get it from? And how will I know if it's any good?'

The young man shook his head. 'In my own country I might be able to advise you; here, I am very unsure. I wonder, *madame*, would you permit me to absent myself for a short time? I would like to purchase a newspaper.'

'Of course,' Eve replied, drawing up the blind and unlocking the door.

After he had gone, she wondered whom she might ask about the wine. The name of Colonel Ballantyne came into her mind, but she dismissed it at once. If he were to appear, then she might be able to ask him casually, but she would no more send him a message or go to see him than fly. He had had enough to say about her conduct before, without her adding any more fuel to the flames.

She was on the point of deciding upon coffee after all — for to serve inferior wine would be worse than to serve none at all — when she was offered a most unexpected solution to her problem. Goodman, who had been despatched to see if he could find a couple of shutters that were missing from one of the windows, came into the bookshop where Eve had been talking with D'Angers a little earlier, to tell her that there was something that might interest her in the cellar.

'Mr Trafford mentioned the cellar to me

when he was taking us round the house,' Eve told him. 'What have you found?'

Goodman led Eve to a trapdoor in a corner of the kitchen.

'What's down there?' Eve asked cautiously, remembering an occasion at her parents' home when she had been invited to go into the cellar by someone standing below, and by the light of a lamp had seen rather a large toad walking about.

Goodman lowered himself through the trapdoor and down the ladder that led from it to the floor below. Moments later, he handed Eve a dusty bottle.

'Wine, ma'am,' he said, grinning.

'I wonder if it's any good,' Eve said, looking at the glass covered with dust from who knew how many years.

Goodman shook his head. 'Don't ask me, ma'am,' he answered. 'I prefer a glass of beer, myself.'

'We need M. D'Angers,' said Eve. 'He has only slipped out for a few minutes. He is bound to be able to tell us: Frenchmen know about wine.' Then, realizing that she had made rather a sweeping statement, she added, 'At least, they ought to.'

D'Angers himself came in at that point, a newspaper in his hand. 'The notice about the opening of the shop has been printed,' he said. 'I have found it today.'

'It should have been in several days ago,' replied Eve, looking down at the bottle. 'People may have made other arrangements by now.'

'Perhaps,' agreed the Frenchman. 'What do you have there, *madame?*'

'Wine,' replied Eve, setting the bottle on the table and wiping her dusty hands on a cloth. 'Goodman found it in the cellar.'

At that moment, the doorbell rang. Goodman's head appeared at the trapdoor, his face wearing an expression of consternation. 'That's the shop door, ma'am,' he said. 'I can't go like this.'

'It's all right. I'll go,' Eve answered, quickly taking off her dirty apron. 'I let up the blind for a few minutes and see what happens? M. D'Angers, will you help Goodman with the wine?'

'You don't want it all got out, do you, ma'am?' asked Goodman.

'No, no, of course not,' Eve replied, as she left the kitchen. 'Just one or two bottles.'

To her surprise, her visitor was Victoria Mirfield, and she bade her a polite greeting, very conscious that her hands were still rather grubby.

'Mrs Scorer, I felt that I must come to see you and return your books,' said the young lady. 'At least,' she amended carefully, 'the ones that are not on their way to China.'

'China!' exclaimed Eve.

'Yes, I had forgotten that you did not know,' answered Miss Mirfield. 'Anyway, I have brought back the — '

'The history book?' Eve enquired humorously.

'It is here,' said Miss Mirfield, handing it to Eve, who set it down on a table next to them. 'I have every intention of attending the opening of your shop next week, and felt that I would enjoy it very much more if I did not have your books on my conscience.'

'You are very kind,' answered Eve. 'Surely you have not come alone?'

'Oh no, indeed,' Victoria assured her. 'My friend, Miss Eagles, is related to the vicar of St James's, so she has called in there first, and intends to meet me here.'

'I see,' Eve replied, wondering why the two young ladies had not made both visits together.

'I can see that you are wondering why I have not gone to the vicarage,' said Miss Mirfield reading Eve's mind. 'The fact of the matter is that when we were together at a seminary in Islington, I persuaded Belinda, the vicar's daughter, to climb over the wall with me so that we could meet . . . well

192

'. . . someone. So the vicar thinks that I lead her into bad ways and he disapproves of me.'

'I am sure you have learned better over the years, Miss Mirfield,' Eve remarked, trying not to laugh.

'Oh yes,' Victoria replied virtuously, though whether she meant that her behaviour had improved, or that her cunning had increased it would have been difficult to tell. 'Are you alone today, Mrs Scorer?'

'M. D'Angers is here, and the servants, of course. Miss Sparrow has taken my son for a walk.'

As if the mention of his name had conjured him up, the young Frenchman appeared from the back of the shop with a tray on which reposed a bottle and some glasses. 'I have brought this so that we can try — ' He stopped suddenly at the sight of the young lady who had just arrived. 'Miss Mirfield!' he exclaimed, then put the tray down and executed an elegant bow.

'M. D'Angers,' replied that young lady, dropping a demure curtsy. 'I hope you are well.'

'I am very well, thank you,' replied the Frenchman. 'Miss Mirfield is a very enthusiastic reader,' he added, turning to Eve. 'She would come here to change her books, oh, many times.'

'I hope you will continue to make use of this establishment,' Eve said warmly.

'I'm sure I shall,' answered Miss Mirfield. Then, in a rather diffident tone, she said 'Mrs Scorer, I do not know how to say this, but there is a smut on your nose.'

'Oh dear,' exclaimed Eve, putting her hand to her face. 'That must be from handling that dusty bottle. Please excuse me for a moment.'

She left the room, then paused briefly outside the door. She should not really leave Miss Mirfield and M. D'Angers alone. Then she consoled herself by reflecting that it would only take her a few moments to remedy her appearance. After all, she was not the keeper of either of those two people. Furthermore, they would be standing in what amounted to the front room of a shop, in a place that was subject to public scrutiny, especially with the blind up.

On looking in the mirror, she saw that there was indeed a mark on her face and she hastened to wash it off. It was only as she was drying her face and hands, however, that it occurred to her that when Victoria had drawn her attention to the mark, she had put her hands up to her face. The smut might have been invented by Victoria, and put there by herself later so that she, Victoria would have an excuse for a tête-à-tête with D'Angers, who had, on his own admission, met the young lady many times.

Then she thought about the Frenchman's start of surprise when he had seen Victoria. It had been very authentic, but if he had really not expected to see her, why had he put three glasses on the tray?

These reflections convinced Eve that she should not leave the young couple unchaperoned for a moment longer than was necessary, and she hurried down the stairs. She was halfway down the flight when she heard the shop door open. That would be Miss Eagles, she decided. But when she entered the shop, she saw that the newcomer was Colonel Ballantyne, and he was not looking very pleased.

'Colonel Ballantyne,' she murmured, curtsying.

'Mrs Scorer,' he replied. 'D'Angers.'

An awkward silence fell, only to be broken by the clang of the bell as the door opened and a tall, rather awkward girl came hurrying in saying, 'Did you manage to — ?' Then, on realizing exactly who was present, she blushed painfully and exclaimed, 'Oh Lord! Oh Victoria I am sorry, I didn't dream . . . that is to say . . . Good morning, Colonel Ballantyne!'

'Good morning, Miss Eagles,' Ballantyne

responded. 'D'Angers, would you be so good as to take my ward and her friend for a little constitutional around the Green? I have a matter of business to discuss with Mrs Scorer.'

The two young ladies could not believe their luck, both at escaping a reprimand, at least for the time being, and at being allowed to promenade with a handsome Frenchman, and they disappeared from the shop at quite unimaginable speed with D'Angers in tow.

'And now, Mrs Scorer,' said the colonel, leaning on his stick in such a way as to bend towards her in rather a menacing way, 'Kindly explain yourself. What the devil were you about, leaving my cousin alone with that popinjay? Believe me, ma'am, though you are at liberty to play foolish games with your own reputation, I'm damned if I'll let you ruin my cousin's.'

14

For a moment or two, Eve stared at Ballantyne in wrathful silence. Then, once she was sure of being in command of her voice, she said, 'I am not accustomed to playing games with my reputation, sir, regardless of what you might think. Furthermore, I was not aware that chaperoning your cousin was part of my duties. Naively, perhaps, I would have supposed that that was *your* responsibility.'

He flushed. 'That is certainly the case,' he agreed. 'Unfortunately, I was detained briefly before arriving here to meet her and her friend. I assumed that a lady proprietor would have had rather more care for her customers.'

'The shop is not yet open,' Eve responded defensively.

'In which case your responsibility is all the greater, for this establishment is by way of still being a private dwelling,' the colonel retorted. 'Would you have left a young lady alone with a gentleman in your own drawing room?'

'I am not a chaperon,' Eve declared again,

uncomfortably aware that she herself had felt uneasy about leaving Miss Mirfield alone with D'Angers. 'Nor is M. D'Angers a popinjay. Just because he does not peacock around in a scarlet coat does not mean that he is to be despised.' She was rather pleased with this speech, but unfortunately, she then spoiled the effect by adding, 'Besides, there was a smut on my nose.'

Ballantyne's brows had drawn together during this last speech. Now he said 'What?' in tones of utter bafflement.

'There was a smut on my nose,' Eve repeated. 'I could not entertain guests in such a condition.'

The colonel stared at her, then to her surprise, burst out laughing, his expression lightening in a most unexpected way. 'I can almost hear my mother saying the same thing. To be fair, my cousin's ability to evade chaperons is legendary.'

'In that case, sir, I wonder that you allowed yourself to be detained elsewhere, however briefly,' Eve said forthrightly.

'Perhaps it was a mistake on my part,' he said, disconcerting her. 'I must say, I'd give something to know who told you that there was a smut on your nose.'

She coloured. 'It was quite true, sir, I assure you.'

He inclined his head slightly. 'I did not doubt it, ma'am,' he said.

Belatedly remembering her manners, Eve invited her visitor to be seated. 'You must be tired,' she said.

'You are very good, particularly in view of my behaviour last time I was here.'

'You acknowledge, then, that you were at fault,' she said, her chin up.

'I spoke immoderately, and with too much haste,' he responded. 'Sometimes my injury pains me and I become short-tempered as a result. Will you forgive me?'

There was a moment of complete stillness which seemed to last for much longer than it really did. Then the clanging of the doorbell broke the silence, and Miss Sparrow and Luke stood on the threshold.

'In a good hour,' Eve declared. 'Miss Sparrow, I must make Colonel Ballantyne known to you. Luke, come and make your bow.'

Luke's eyes grew very wide. 'Colonel Blazes!' he breathed.

Ballantyne had risen at their entrance and now he bowed gravely. 'At your service, Miss Sparrow,' he said. 'Master Scorer, I would have known you anywhere. You have very much a look of your papa.' To Eve, who was more accustomed to hearing harsh, disapproving tones from him the gentleness of his voice was a revelation. It was as if a roaring lion had suddenly started purring.

'Mama says I am like him,' the boy replied, an expression of blatant hero-worship in his eyes. He was clearly unafraid of this man who must look like a giant to him. 'I have a picture, but it's only a miniature. Mama says he was very brave.'

'Yes, he was,' replied the colonel. 'You can be very proud of him.'

'That's what Mama says,' answered Luke. 'She showed me his medals.'

'He can be very proud of his mama, too,' put in Miss Sparrow. 'You know that I am a general's daughter, Colonel, and therefore I value the courage of our fighting men very highly. It takes another sort of courage to remain at home waiting for news, scrimping and saving and having to depend upon the charity of relations.'

Ballantyne glanced quickly at Eve, and saw that she had flushed a little.

'You make too much of it, Lavinia,' she replied.

'On the contrary, I think I probably make too little of it,' replied the older lady tranquilly. 'Shall I take Luke upstairs now?'

'Yes, please,' answered Eve.

'A fine boy,' the colonel remarked after Luke had gone, but only after Ballantyne had promised to call again very soon.

'I think so,' Eve agreed softly.

'You have not said whether you have forgiven me,' he reminded her.

'Of course I have,' she said frankly. 'You have very properly reminded me that you were injured in the service of your country. Any man who has suffered in such a way must command my respect and my sympathy. I should have been more attentive to your needs, Colonel.'

'Not at all,' he replied briefly, writhing inwardly.

After a brief silence Eve said in tones of some confusion, 'As Luke was speaking about his father's miniature, I was reminded of something. Edmund had a picture of me of a similar size, which I believe he kept amongst his belongings.' She flushed. 'Forgive me, Colonel. I know you would have returned it if you had it.'

It was the colonel's turn to flush. 'No, Mrs Scorer, I do have it,' he answered her. 'There was some trifling damage to the frame, which is being mended. By your leave, I will bring it next time I come.'

'That is very good of you,' she replied. 'I should like Luke to have the two.'

'Are you comfortable here?' he asked her abruptly after another silence. 'Are you served well? Who works for you, for instance?'

Inwardly, he cursed his sharp tone, his lack of smoothness. Eve did not seem to notice but merely said, 'I am well looked after, thank you. Goodman you know, and Mrs Castle and her daughter. Todd is less useful, but he is an old soldier. His wife works well.'

'And D'Angers?'

'D'Angers knows his work. Is this an interrogation, Colonel?'

'No, of course not,' he replied shortly. Then to change the subject, he gestured towards the bottle of wine which D'Angers had placed on the table. 'Is handling this what made you soil your face?' he asked her. 'It was done in a very good cause, if so.'

Eve stared at him, her eyes opening wide. 'You are very shrewd, sir,' she remarked. 'Yes, Goodman has just discovered this.'

'Discovered it?' he echoed.

'We had not looked in the cellar before today. It turns out to have wine in it.'

'That is very intriguing. Have you brought this out in order to taste it?'

Eve nodded. 'That had been my intention,' she admitted. 'I was thinking of serving wine at the opening of my bookshop, but was not sure how to go about buying it, or even how to be certain that what I was buying was worth the money.'

'The discovery of this wine in your very own cellar would appear to have solved your problem,' the colonel answered. He picked up the bottle in order to study it.

'Only in part,' Eve said diffidently. 'I don't know whether it's any good, you see.' She paused briefly. 'Do you know anything about wine, Colonel Ballantyne?'

He grinned. For the second time that day, she noticed how attractive his rather harsh-featured face became when he smiled. 'Pass me the corkscrew, Mrs Scorer,' he said. He removed the cork expertly, held it to his nose and sniffed thoughtfully. Then he poured the wine into two glasses, and offered her one. She took it, but waited whilst he raised his glass to his lips.

'Well?' she asked impatiently, when he said nothing.

He looked at her solemnly and shook his head. 'You must not on any account serve this at the opening of your shop, ma'am,' he said firmly.

'Is it not acceptable?' she asked anxiously.

'Acceptable is not the right word,' he responded. 'It is quite outstanding, and far too good for your customers.' He took another mouthful, rolled it round and swallowed appreciatively.

Eve sipped from her own glass. She was no

expert but even she could tell that this was quite out of the ordinary. 'What is to be done, then?' she asked him. 'It is all very well to say that I should not serve this wine, but it is to hand, and I shall not have to pay for it. If I do not use this, I shall have to purchase some other, and I will still have the problem of not knowing where to get it from.'

'Allow me to suggest a possible solution,' said the colonel. 'If you let me have, say, a case of this wine for my own use, I will be happy to provide the wine for your event from my cellar.'

'Oh no, that is far too much, sir,' Eve exclaimed.

'Forgive me, but I think that a case for my efforts would be perfectly reasonable,' Ballantyne replied mildly.

She coloured. 'No, sir, I meant that it would be too much to expect you to provide all the wine for my customers' consumption.'

'Permit me to be the judge of that,' he responded. 'Besides, I owe you something else in compensation for my ward's failure to return that volume of poetry by Mr Southey.'

'Wine for a party in exchange for a mere book!' she exclaimed.

'Yes, but there are other advantages on my side,' he told her.

'Indeed?' she questioned, raising her brows.

'You will feel obliged to me,' he remarked. 'Your good health, Mrs Scorer!'

Eve had no idea how she should reply to this. His words clearly indicated a desire to flirt with her, but his tone was rather too matter-of-fact for dalliance. She found it hard to reconcile this with his earlier disapproval of her. On the other hand, if he thought her a woman of doubtful morals, he probably thought that flirting was all she was good for!

Before she could think further about this disturbing idea, however, the door which led to the kitchen quarters opened and Mrs Castle appeared. 'Colonel Ballantyne!' she exclaimed. 'Oh, Colonel Ballantyne!' She dropped a reverent curtsy and, as she looked up, the expression on her face would not have been inappropriate had she just witnessed the performance of a miracle by Our Lord Himself.

'Mrs Castle,' replied the colonel, with a smile. 'What a pleasure to see you here, and so happily situated. Is Joanna well?'

'Oh yes indeed, sir, and we are so happy here, as you say,' she beamed. 'When I heard the other day that I had missed you, I was so disappointed. But Mrs Scorer assured me that you would be back soon, and I see that she was right.'

'Naturally,' he murmured.

Mrs Castle glanced from Eve to the colonel and back again, and her eye kindled. 'Oh, so that's the way of it, is it? Well, I couldn't be more pleased.'

'Mrs Castle,' protested Eve, in some consternation.

'I'll just go and get some of my special biscuits,' she said, bowing herself out of the room as if leaving the presence of royalty.

'How could you?' Eve demanded of Ballantyne. 'She now has the impression that . . . that . . . '

'Yes, Mrs Scorer?' the colonel prompted, one eyebrow raised, his head tilted a little to one side.

'Her impression is quite mistaken,' said Eve firmly, her colour rather high.

'And what impression would that be?' he asked her blandly.

'You know very well what impression that would be,' she said crossly. 'Well she is mistaken and that is all that is to be said on the matter.'

'I cannot see how you can be so certain of that,' the colonel replied. 'After all, the inference to be drawn from Mrs Castle's remarks would surely be that *I* have an interest in *you*, and you are in no position either to confirm or to deny that, are you?'

Eve stared at him in amazement. Twice

within one conversation he had expressed a desire to know her better. Was he flirting? Why had he decided to do so now? Before she could make any response, even had she been able to think of anything to say, which was rather unlikely under the circumstances, the outside door opened and Miss Mirfield, Miss Eagles and D'Angers came in, talking and laughing about something that they had seen in the street. Eve was not sorry that the moment was lost. She was not at all sure how she would have responded to Ballantyne's remarks.

'Ah, you have opened the wine!' exclaimed D'Angers. 'And what is your opinion, *m'sieur?*'

Ballantyne's response was to gesture towards the bottle and the spare glass with an open hand. The Frenchman poured himself a small amount into the bottom of a glass, smelled it, then drank. '*Madame*,' he said, turning to Eve after an appreciative pause, 'you cannot possibly serve this to your customers.'

'You echo my words exactly,' put in the colonel.

'May we have some?' Miss Mirfield asked.

'Certainly not,' replied Ballantyne. 'This is not to be wasted on silly chits of girls. If you ask very nicely, Mrs Scorer may procure you some lemonade.'

'Oh, all right,' responded Victoria not noticeably dashed. 'I think all red wine tastes like ink anyway.'

The colonel briefly covered his eyes with his hand then said to D'Angers, 'You must forgive my cousin, sir. She has no palate at all, I fear.'

The Frenchman smiled. 'I believe in this country you have a saying: 'All the more for the rest of us',' he replied.

'So we do,' Ballantyne agreed, filling the Frenchman's glass then his own, after offering Eve more, which she refused.

Mrs Castle came in shortly afterwards with a plate of biscuits, and a jug of lemonade, for she had heard the young ladies return and had anticipated the colonel's suggestion, and for a time they made a merry party. Miss Eagles and Miss Mirfield spent some time looking at the books on the shelves, and talking eagerly about the things that they had read. Colonel Ballantyne chatted briefly with Mrs Castle before talking very easily with D'Angers about wine and the grape-growing regions of France. Eve, as the hostess, hovered between the conversations. She could not help noticing how Miss Mirfield's gaze often strayed towards the young Frenchman. She recalled how the younger woman had responded to Hadleigh's attentions. She was plainly something of a flirt, and Ballantyne had his hands full keeping an eye on her.

She hoped that D'Angers would not be hurt. She had a feeling that he was less practised in the art of flirtation than the colonel's ward. He was inclined to be earnest, and she was afraid that he might take the whole business far too seriously. She could not imagine that the colonel would contemplate a match between Miss Mirfield and a penniless shop assistant with complaisance.

Eventually, the colonel announced that it was time that they should be leaving. 'Send Goodman round to tell me when it's convenient to bring the wine,' he said as he rose, wincing a little. 'I would suggest a couple of days before the event, to give it time to settle. My men can bring back a case of your wine when they return.'

Miss Mirfield's eyes sparkled. 'You are providing Mrs Scorer with wine for her party?'

Ballantyne nodded. 'In exchange for some of this excellent vintage from her cellar. Until the opening of the shop, then, ma'am.'

'But we may meet before then, may we not?' said Miss Mirfield. 'Why do we not get up an expedition to, say, Bagnigge Wells? It's not as fashionable as it once was, but it's only a short drive away.'

'Bagnigge Wells?' Eve echoed. 'What a strange name.'

'Would you like to go, ma'am?' the colonel asked her. 'There are some pretty gardens there, which I believe your son would like, and the waters are beneficial, I understand.'

'It was a favourite resort of Charles II and Nell Gwynne,' put in Miss Mirfield helpfully.

'There you are, Mrs Scorer,' murmured the colonel. 'In that case, how can you refuse?'

Eve contented herself with a challenging look.

★   ★   ★

On the day of the proposed expedition, Eve dressed in an outfit that she had not previously worn, a lavender-grey carriage dress with black piping around the hem and the sleeves. She had surveyed herself in her full-length mirror before leaving the house, and decided that she might not be as beautiful as Miss Mirfield, but on this occasion, she would be every bit as stylish. Luke had been very excited when he had been told about the expedition, and was looking forward to driving with Colonel Blazes.

'Will he be wearing his uniform, Mama?' he asked Eve. They were ready in good time, and waiting in the shop, looking out for the carriage so that the colonel would not have to keep his horses standing.

'I don't suppose so, darling,' Eve answered him, her heart swelling with pride at the sight of the sturdy little boy. One of the most agreeable consequences of her new affluence, in her opinion, was the fact that she could now afford to dress Luke well and provide for his future.

'I *want* him to wear his uniform,' protested Luke. 'Why won't he be wearing it?'

'Because he is leaving the army.'

'Why?'

'Because of his wounded leg.'

Luke was silent for a few moments, his brow wrinkled in thought. 'Will he have his sword?'

'I don't know,' Eve replied.

'I 'spect he's the best at sword fighting in the whole world, don't you, Mama?'

'I expect so,' Eve responded, her eye caught by a pile of books that someone had knocked into disarray.

'He's very big and strong, isn't he?'

'Yes, he is,' Eve agreed, as she straightened the books. She would have to speak to D'Angers about leaving things so untidily.

'And brave.'

'Mm.'

'Joanna thinks he's handsome. Do *you* think he's handsome, Mama?'

At that moment the barouche drew up outside, containing Colonel Ballantyne and his ward. Miss Sparrow, who had gone upstairs to collect her shawl, came down, and they all hurried outside to save the colonel from having to get down and come to the door.

'Good afternoon,' said Ballantyne, as the groom leaped down from his place and opened the door for the ladies and Luke. 'We have a fine day for our drive.' The colonel was sitting with his back to the horses, whilst Miss Mirfield had taken the corner diagonally opposite him.

'Colonel Blazes, Colonel Blazes!' Luke cried. 'Mama and I think you're the biggest, bravest, strongest and most handsomest man in the whole world, don't we, Mama? *And* the best at sword-fighting.' The little boy's piping tones meant that his remarks were audible to all the assembled party, as well as to half the street.

'"Most handsome" or "handsomest",' corrected Miss Sparrow carefully. 'There is no need to use both.'

'But he *is* the most handsomest,' Luke insisted. 'Mama said so.'

'I am sure your mama would never express

herself ungrammatically,' said the colonel tranquilly. 'Shall we go?'

Eve could feel her face burning, and she could not meet Ballantyne's eye. She would have liked to correct the false impression that Luke's comments had made, but could not think how to do so without being rude.

'I would simply let the subject drop, if I were you,' said Ballantyne under his breath as she sat down opposite him, whilst Luke and Miss Sparrow sat opposite Miss Mirfield. 'Small children have an unparalleled ability for embarrassing one, I find, and the more one tries to stop them, the worse it gets.'

'You are right, of course,' Eve agreed, wondering nevertheless how she could correct the impression that she and her son had been exchanging superlatives concerning the colonel's appearance and prowess.

'If it's any consolation, I'm sure you don't really think I'm handsome,' Ballantyne assured her.

'Oh, but — ' She stopped suddenly, realizing that in her haste not to seem unkind she was falling into a trap that the colonel had very neatly set for her. He laughed, and seeing his tanned face, the corners of his eyes crinkled with amusement, his eyes lit up, and his mouth set in a generous curve, she realized that 'handsome' might not be an entirely inappropriate epithet after all. In fact, he cut a very fine figure in his dark-blue coat, buckskin breeches and shiny boots. She recalled Mrs Castle saying that as a serving army officer he had turned heads. Remembering him dressed in his regimentals and picturing him mounted on horseback, she could well believe it.

Realizing that she had barely spoken to Miss Mirfield beyond exchanging a greeting, she turned to converse with her, whilst Luke eagerly observed the passing scene, asking questions which almost invariably began 'Colonel Blazes'.

The drive was a pleasant one, taking them away from the centre of London and into a more rural area. It was not a long journey, however, and Eve found herself thinking that even Luke could have walked the distance quite easily. She was about to say so when she realized how tactless it would be to make such a remark in front of Colonel Ballantyne. How irksome he must find his disability! She deliberately looked away when he got down from the barouche. She had no wish to humiliate him by observing the clumsiness forced upon him by his injury.

If the colonel did grit his teeth when he climbed down, it was not from pain but from annoyance. The bruising on his leg no longer pained him, and he was now quite capable of taking part in all his usual pursuits. Had he been in London in the normal way of things, he would have been riding in the park every day before breakfast, sparring regularly at Jackson's boxing saloon, and fencing at Angelo's. As it was, all these activities were denied him, thanks to his agreement with Pitt.

He was a man who enjoyed vigorous exercise, and he found the restrictions which his subterfuge had imposed upon him irksome in the extreme. His batman was privy to his secrets, so at least he was able to relax in the privacy of his own bedroom. It was there that he did fifty press-ups every morning, to keep his muscles in good condition.

He was not made to be a spy, he decided, as they began to stroll about the gardens, the rest of the party carefully measuring their pace so as not to hurry him. He loathed subterfuge. That was why he had never really taken a great deal of pleasure in London society. People there were very much inclined to say one thing and mean another. He liked matters to be straightforward. What was all the more aggravating, he felt that he had learned precious little.

'Colonel Blazes, can we go and play

skittles?' asked Luke, as soon as his feet had touched the ground. 'You said that we might!'

'I said that your mama must decide,' Ballantyne insisted.

'But she is sure to say yes! Can we?'

''May we',' corrected Miss Sparrow automatically. 'I expect your mama would like to stroll about the gardens a little first.'

'Yes, I should,' Eve agreed. 'I am told that there is a fountain with a boy and a swan with water coming out of his beak. Wouldn't you like to see that, Luke?'

'Yes, I should,' Luke agreed, 'but not as much as I would like to play skittles.'

Ballantyne laughed. 'I'll take him to play skittles, and perhaps Miss Sparrow would come with me. If you two ladies would like to stroll about a little, shall we meet at the fountain in, say, an hour, then go and have some tea?'

They all agreed to this suggestion, and soon Eve and Victoria were taking a leisurely walk around the gardens, admiring the grotto and the many curious shrubs and flowers.

'Is this a favourite haunt of yours, Miss Mirfield?' Eve asked her companion. Miss Mirfield was dressed in a celestial blue walking dress with a charming straw bonnet trimmed with blue and white flowers, and Eve was glad that her own attire was

216

becoming and fashionable, if of a more sober hue.

'Not really. I usually go to Hyde Park, but I thought that this would be more enjoyable for your son, and also more accessible for Jason.'

'You're quite right,' Eve agreed. 'Luke could not wait to get to the skittles. I only hope that he will not tire Colonel Ballantyne too much.'

'Oh, Jason can stand up for himself. How old is your son, Mrs Scorer? Do you intend to send him to school?'

Eve was just telling her companion about how she planned to send Luke to Rugby, which was the school that Edmund had attended, when she broke off as her eyes took in a most unwelcome sight. Coming towards them were Julia Comberton accompanied by Horace Bunty.

Her first instinct was to run in the opposite direction. She had not seen Horace since he had pinned her to the wall and kissed her against her will, and she had no desire to encounter him again. As for Julia, she had resigned herself to meeting her from the moment she had discovered that her cousin was in London. Her heart sank at the prospect of encountering one who had treated her as something a little lower than a scullery maid.

A meeting now seemed inevitable, however,

and, as they drew closer, Eve could see that Julia was, if possible, even less pleased to see her than she was to see Julia.

'Well, this is delightful,' murmured Horace Bunty, at almost the same time as Mrs Comberton was saying, 'What upon earth are you doing here?'

'I'm glad I see you well, Cousin,' Eve replied, determined not to descend to the same level. 'May I make Miss Mirfield known to you?'

'I am already acquainted with Miss Mirfield,' her cousin replied haughtily. 'I had no idea that *you* were, however.'

'Miss Mirfield is Colonel Ballantyne's cousin,' Eve answered, determined to be courteous to Julia, even if her cousin did not accord her the same kindness. 'Colonel Ballantyne was Edmund's commanding officer.'

'Oh, was he? Do you know the gardens well, Miss Mirfield?' Julia's deliberate rudeness with regard to Eve's concerns was no surprise to her cousin, but Eve could see that Victoria was rather taken aback, and therefore failed to answer Julia's question.

'I certainly hope so,' remarked Bunty, stepping into the breach, 'for it was upon Miss Mirfield's recommendation that I brought you here today, ma'am.'

'I have heard about them, of course, and

they are much more agreeable than I expected,' Julia observed. 'I am sure that somebody told me they were only frequented by tradesmen and their families now and had become quite low and common.' She paused infinitesimally, then covered her mouth in rather an artificial manner. 'Of course I did not mean you, Eve,' she said. 'You have hardly been in business for long enough to acquire the smell of the shop.'

'I think that the London air has had a very becoming effect upon Mrs Scorer,' said Bunty as he looked at Eve approvingly.

'Say rather the effect of new gowns,' Julia corrected, looking Eve up and down. Although they had both been widowed at approximately the same time, Julia had cast off her mourning completely and was now in a walking gown of cherry red, whereas Eve was still in half-mourning.

'Well, you must know that as well as I,' Eve answered in an even tone.

Julia flushed. 'I am sure I am not to blame if while you were living with us you chose to spend every penny you had on Luke.'

Very conscious that this conversation could easily descend into a family squabble, Eve said, 'I expect most women make a good deal of fuss of their sons, given the opportunity.'

'Only if they want to spoil them,' said Julia

tartly. 'Shall we walk?'

Given the choice of either Horace Bunty or Julia Comberton to walk with, Eve would have been hard put to it to decide which she would have liked the least. If she were honest, she would infinitely have preferred to say goodbye to them both and continue her walk with Victoria, and she could see by the stormy look on her cousin's face that Julia was of the same mind. Short of running in the opposite direction, though, escape would appear to be impossible, so she resolved that in so far as it lay within her power, the whole party should keep together.

In the event, it appeared that Horace Bunty had decided that he would walk with Eve, whilst Julia and Victoria strolled ahead. Although he held out his arm to her, she did not take it, choosing instead to walk with her hands behind her back. He did not labour the point, and walked beside her, saying, 'My parents would like to be remembered to you.'

'That is kind of them,' Eve replied. 'Pray send them my best wishes when you next communicate with them.'

'I am not sure when that will be,' he told her. 'I intend to remain in London for the present.'

Her heart sank. 'Your parents will miss

you,' she remarked, keeping her tone indifferent.

'Possibly; but I have pressing reasons for being here. Perhaps you might guess what they are.'

'No doubt matters of business.'

'Mrs Scorer, do not be so disingenuous. You cannot think how distressed I was to discover that you had left your cousin's home.'

'I very much doubt that, sir,' she said.

'Oh come, ma'am, stop fencing with me,' he said in a low urgent tone. 'You know perfectly well that I intend to have you, and that it is only a matter of time before I achieve my objective. Your removal to London merely postpones the inevitable.'

Eve stopped in her tracks. 'Your conceit beggars belief,' she declared. Julia and Victoria were walking on a short way ahead, oblivious to the contretemps that was taking place behind them.

'It's hardly conceited to have a proper understanding of my own worth,' he replied calmly. 'You're a widow with a brat. No man is going to want to take on another's child, so marriage is out of the question, and you don't have enough of this world's good to tempt anyone.'

'Really?' Eve replied calmly. 'I would have

thought that ten thousand pounds would be quite a substantial temptation.'

'Ten thousand pounds?' Bunty echoed, his expression one of astonishment. Clearly this was news to him. 'You cannot tell me that your shop is worth that much.'

'I was left the shop *and* ten thousand pounds,' Eve told him, smiling cynically. 'Were you not informed? Perhaps Julia forgot about that.'

He paused. 'No, I was not informed. You are right, then; your fortune does indeed constitute a temptation. I can see that I must look out for rivals.'

Eve could not believe it. Could he really imagine that she was foolish enough to be taken in by him? She could not answer for disgust. She was pleased, therefore, when coming towards them she saw the elegant, willowy figure of Max Hadleigh.

'Mr Hadleigh!' she exclaimed when the party were all together, Julia and Victoria having stopped to greet the newcomer. 'How delightful to see you here! Have you come to take the waters?'

'Mrs Scorer!' he answered, with a smile that held a hint of surprise at the warmth of her greeting. 'Delightful indeed! And Miss Mirfield too! But I do not think that I have met your companions.'

Eve made haste to introduce her cousin and Mr Bunty. She noticed how gratified Julia was to meet one whose name was known in fashionable circles and she was conscious of an unworthy feeling of satisfaction that she should have been the one to perform this introduction.

'Will you not join us, Mr Hadleigh?' Julia suggested. 'We were just having a stroll about the gardens.'

'Yes, please do,' Eve said quickly, conscious that she was acting a little out of character. 'I would like to consult you about the decoration for my shop. I want everything to look fashionable.'

If Mr Hadleigh was surprised, he did not say so, but readily offered Eve his arm. Julia fell into step with them, which meant that Eve was obliged to ask Hadleigh all kinds of questions about mirrors, tables, curtains and wall-coverings. She hoped that he did not later ask her about his answers, or, worse still, expect to see his recommendations carried out, for more than half of her mind was taken with thinking about Horace Bunty, and how she could convince him of her lack of interest in him. The rest of it was hoping that she was not giving Hadleigh too much encouragement, but between the two men, she felt that the London dandy was probably the lesser of the two evils.

This time Bunty walked behind, conversing politely with Victoria, and keeping his eyes on Eve. He had desired her from the moment she had come to live with her cousin. He had thought initially that because she was a poor relation with no prospects, she would be an easy conquest. This had proved not to be the case. Julia's unkindness might have driven other women to seek for comfort elsewhere, but not Eve Scorer. Her resistance to his advances had only made him desire her the more. Furthermore, the presence of Max Hadleigh had given him pause, for he had not expected to have a rival. He had not previously thought of offering her marriage, but ten thousand pounds was a powerful inducement, especially in view of the fact that his father had said he would not settle any more of his debts. The business in Clerkenwell would be worth something as well. Then he would be able to tell his father to go hang, and enjoy himself in fashionable London as he had always wished to do.

In her anxiety to avoid further conversation with Bunty, Eve failed to keep an eye on the time, and consequently when the moment came for their rendezvous with Ballantyne, Luke and Miss Sparrow, they were a little distance away from the fountain.

'What's five or ten minutes?' drawled Julia. 'They can very well wait.'

'I'm afraid five or ten minutes is a good deal to a small boy,' Eve responded, 'and we must not keep Miss Sparrow waiting.'

'It's also a good deal to a colonel of dragoons,' Victoria added with feeling.

The party made their way to the fountain and saw that the other three were already waiting. Ballantyne's lips tightened a little when he saw the new members of the party.

'Mama, Mama!' said Luke hurrying forward. 'I have been playing skittles with Colonel Blazes.'

'I see your manners have not improved,' remarked Julia coldly. 'Where is your greeting for me, and for Mr Bunty?'

Luke stopped in his tracks. He had not seen Bunty until that moment. 'Good morning, Aunt Julia,' he said expressionlessly. 'Good morning, Mr Bunty.'

'Well done, Luke,' said Eve with an encouraging smile. 'Mr Hadleigh, this is my son Luke. Luke, make your bow.'

The boy did so, then said, 'We wondered where you were, Mama.'

'Your mama has been keeping herself very well amused, obviously,' said the colonel gravely. 'You must not mind if she is a little late.'

'You must blame us for the delay, Colonel Ballantyne,' Julia murmured, fluttering her eyelashes.

'I'm sure it was no one's fault,' Ballantyne replied evenly.

'You are too gracious, sir. I am sure if I were late on parade you would have some fearsome punishment to administer.' Again, she looked up at him flirtatiously.

He smiled at her politely. 'Fortunately, I am no longer in the military, so that is not an eventuality with which you need to concern yourself.'

'What a pity,' she purred. 'I should have enjoyed playing the penitent.'

He looked a little uncomfortable and cleared his throat. 'Shall we go and have some tea?'

Eve's heart sank at the idea of sitting down to tea with this motley collection of individuals, but, fortunately, Bunty had other ideas. Eve was his object, but Julia was also his mistress, and he had no desire to sit watching her flirt with Ballantyne under his nose.

'We already have an engagement, I fear,' he said, firmly taking hold of Julia's arm. Max Hadleigh also had a commitment elsewhere, so it was just the original party who walked together to the tea room. Luke ran on ahead, with Victoria just behind, showing that she had only recently left her schoolgirl days behind. Miss Sparrow walked briskly after them, leaving Ballantyne and Eve to bring up the rear.

'I have a word of advice for you, ma'am,' said the colonel, as they walked along.

'Now why should I have the feeling that this is going to be unpalatable?' Eve asked, as if to herself.

'I have no idea,' Ballantyne answered. 'Possibly because in the past your actions have frequently been such that those responsible for you have been obliged to criticize your behaviour?'

'Strangely enough that has not been the case,' Eve responded, keeping a rein on her temper with some difficulty. 'In fact, you are the only one who has consistently criticized my behaviour, and with very little justification, in my opinion.'

'Your cousin Julia — ' Ballantyne began.

'Oh yes, my cousin Julia,' Eve interrupted, her tone deceptively pleasant. 'Does it not strike you as a little ironic that you should be censuring me, whilst at the same time indulging Julia with a flirtation that was enough to put any decent woman to the blush? Now, unless I am to be so unmannerly as to kick your stick from beneath you and leave you to make your way to the tea room as well as you might without it, may I suggest that you keep your presumptuous opinions to yourself?'

The colonel smiled grimly. 'Very well, ma'am, but do not blame me if Mr Bunty loses patience with you and finds someone else to pursue.' Eve halted, turned to the colonel and drew a deep breath, but before she could say anything he spoke again. 'Please do not attempt to deprive me of my stick. I may be incapacitated to some degree, but I am quite capable of dealing with recalcitrant females. I should hate young Luke to have to witness the spectacle of his mama being put across my knee and soundly spanked!'

Eve made an infuriated sound and walked on ahead, to where the other three were waiting, fortunately only a short distance away.

The colonel ordered tea and cakes for them, and took up the offer of lemonade for Luke. Miss Sparrow asked Miss Mirfield about other visits that she had made to the gardens in the past. Thankfully, their conversation was such that Ballantyne and Eve were able to join in from time to time without drawing attention to the fact that neither one was talking to the other.

The cakes, when they arrived, proved to be of such a size as to meet with the approval of a small boy, and Luke began to eat his with wholehearted enjoyment. 'I'm glad Mr Bunty didn't stay,' he said during a lull in the conversation. 'I don't like him.'

'I do not think your mama would be pleased to hear you say that,' the colonel suggested.

'She doesn't like him either,' he replied.

'Luke, don't talk with your mouth full,' said Eve.

'My mouth isn't full,' he answered truthfully. 'Anyway, you *don't* like him. You said — '

'Luke!' Eve said again, in outraged tones.

'I like Colonel Blazes much better. Don't you, Mama?'

'More tea, Colonel?' asked Miss Sparrow calmly. 'No more personal remarks please, Luke. Confine your comments to the weather and the surrounding scenery.' Thankfully for Eve's peace of mind, Luke made no more embarrassing observations.

Later as they walked back to the carriage, Eve went on ahead with Luke and Victoria, while the colonel and Miss Sparrow brought up the rear.

'I think I owe you an apology, Mrs Scorer,'

Victoria said, as Luke ran on just out of earshot.

'I am very sure you do not,' Eve replied.

'Yes I do,' Victoria answered. 'You see, it was partly my fault that Mrs Comberton and Mr Bunty were here today.'

'Do not be so critical of yourself,' Eve told her reassuringly. 'All you did was mention where we were going. It was no secret, after all.'

'That's not the whole truth, actually,' Victoria replied in a low tone. 'I met Mr Bunty by chance in Bond Street, yesterday and he was saying how much he wanted to renew his suit to see if you could be prevailed upon to accept him. He asked me if I would help him find an opportunity, and so of course — '

'Of course you told him that I would be here,' Eve concluded for her. 'Well, of all the despicable tricks! I beg your pardon, Miss Mirfield,' she went on quickly, seeing Victoria's startled look. 'I was not referring to you! I mean Bunty! The only suit he has ever tried to press upon me was a dishonourable one.'

Victoria gasped. 'Surely Mrs Comberton would never permit him to escort her if she knew.'

Eve was very sure that her cousin had

designs of her own on Bunty, hence her displeasure earlier. Instead of saying so, she merely offered, 'I think that she did not choose to think such a thing of a near neighbour. He has pursued me to London, now, and may be starting to consider marriage because of my inheritance, but his feelings for me are no more honourable than they ever were. I would be obliged, Miss Mirfield, if you would not engineer any more meetings.'

'No indeed, I would not dream of doing so,' Victoria answered, as they got to the carriage.

Eve invited the colonel and Miss Mirfield in for refreshments when they got back to the shop. They declined, insisting that they were already satisfied with what they had enjoyed at the gardens. 'But we shall see you at the opening of the shop,' said Miss Mirfield.

'If we can find our way in amongst your admirers,' added the colonel.

'Or yours,' Eve retorted swiftly before they drove off.

'That's given you your own,' Victoria observed, as the carriage was pulling away.

'Hold your tongue and stop being vulgar,' he snapped.

Victoria had intended to tell him about what Mrs Scorer had said with regard to Mr

Bunty, but given the mood that her guardian was in, she decided to keep her own counsel, at least for the present. This left the colonel to enjoy his own thoughts in peace.

Enjoyment was possibly the wrong word. The outing had not been one of unalloyed pleasure as far as he was concerned. He was getting very tired of limping everywhere; strangely enough, the assumed uneven gait was having the effect of making his leg ache. He was also getting very tired to being dismissed to the ranks of the elderly and the infantile. Had he been able to walk about the gardens, he would have been there when they encountered Bunty and Hadleigh, and could have seen for himself how Eve reacted to them. Perhaps she had enjoyed flirting first with one, then with another; yet from what he had observed of her behaviour, she did not seem inclined to be flirtatious. Certainly, she had never attempted to flirt with *him*, unlike her cousin Julia. With a flash of insight, he recalled Eve, very properly dressed in half-mourning whilst Julia, widowed for the same length of time paraded about in cherry red. What did that say about the two women? Julia's remarks and behaviour, he was sure, could very easily pass beyond the bounds of decency. What would it be like to flirt with Eve, to exchange teasing glances and remarks charged with innuendo?

He brought himself up with a start. Who was he trying to fool? He was a bluff soldier with no aptitude for such things, as Julia was almost certainly discovering. As for Eve Scorer, no doubt she would put him firmly in his place.

15

'Why Biddy, this is good of you,' Eve exclaimed, as they walked into the shop. Biddy Todd was clearly having a very busy time. She had been taking books off the shelves, dusting them, then also dusting the shelves themselves before putting the books back.

Biddy looked surprised to see them. 'I thought you were all going back to Berkeley Square, ma'am,' she said.

'Not today, Biddy,' Eve responded. Nor any other, she added inwardly, if the colonel was going to use such occasions to make quite unwarranted criticisms of her behaviour! 'I'll just go and put on some old clothes, then I'll come down and help you.'

'There's no need, ma'am,' Biddy answered. 'I don't mind a bit of dusting.'

'Nonsense! Some hard work will do me good.' Eve was about to leave the room when she thought of something else. 'Biddy, were you in the house when Mme Lascelles fell?'

Biddy looked up sharply. 'What makes you ask, ma'am?'

'I thought about it when I was coming

down the stairs the other day.'

'I hope you're careful on those stairs,' Biddy remarked, continuing with her dusting again. 'They're rather steep.'

'Were you here when it happened then?' asked Eve.

'Oh yes, ma'am. I heard the crash and came running through from the kitchen. Broke her neck, she did.'

'Were you alone in the house?'

'Apart from Tim. There was a maidservant that left suddenly a bit before that. Mr D'Angers was around that day, but I'm sure he didn't go upstairs.'

'I don't suppose he would have any reason to,' Eve answered. 'I'll just go and change.' This time it was Biddy's words that called her back.

'That other Frenchman come by earlier, looking for something.'

'M. Monceux?' Eve asked, turning in the doorway. 'Did he say what he wanted?'

'No, ma'am. He just prowled around the shelves a bit and then went.'

'Did he say if he would return? I'm sure we could procure anything for him, if he was wanting something in particular.'

'He didn't say, ma'am. After some of that nasty French stuff, I dare say. I'm told they have a lot of books in France that decent people would blush to read.'

No doubt Colonel Ballantyne would say that that would be just the sort of thing that he would expect to find on her shelves, she mused, as she climbed the stairs.

Miss Sparrow had taken Luke to the kitchen so that he could tell Mrs Castle about the outing. She accompanied Eve upstairs and helped her with changing her gown.

'I just wanted to say, my dear, that I will leave Bunty no opportunity to get you alone if I can help it,' Miss Sparrow said. 'I cannot believe that he has followed you all the way to London!'

'No, neither can I,' Eve agreed.

'If I may make a suggestion . . . ?' ventured Miss Sparrow. Eve looked at her questioningly. 'Ask Colonel Ballantyne for his help. He was Edmund's commanding officer and — '

'And he already has a low opinion of me,' Eve completed angrily. 'Why, I cannot imagine. I am not a saint, but I do not know what I have done to deserve his censure.'

'He has censured you?'

'He never does anything but censure me,' Eve confirmed bitterly. 'I do not know why, but I know that he is the last person to whom I would turn for help — ' She stopped speaking, a lump in her throat. She was determined not to cry.

'I am sorry for it. He would be a powerful protector against such as Horace Bunty. Perhaps if I were to say something — ?'

'Pray do not do so on my account,' Eve interrupted, trying for an airy tone. 'I am surrounded by well-wishers here; yourself, Mrs Castle, Goodman, even the Todds. No doubt Mr Bunty will soon be returning to his father's estate.' She did not repeat what Bunty had said about staying in London. She did not even want to think about it.

* * *

In accordance with Colonel Ballantyne's instructions, Eve sent word to him two days before the opening to say that she was ready to receive the wine. When it arrived the amount that he sent seemed to her to be quite excessive. 'We shall all be drunk as lords if we consume as much as that,' she told M. D'Angers doubtfully.

'It is better to have too much than too little,' he replied with a Gallic shrug.

The day of the opening dawned fine, but dull, which Eve decided was a good omen. 'If it were bright and sunny, people would be tempted to go elsewhere,' she told Miss Sparrow. The question of what to wear had vexed her a little. What exactly did one wear in order to open a shop? She wanted to look business-like, but at the same time, she also wanted to look like a lady. In the end, she put on a stylish but rather severely cut day dress in a dark violet shade. She also dressed her hair in a slightly less elaborate style than she might have adopted for a social engagement.

The invitations had been issued for three o'clock. Eve hesitated for a long time before sending an invitation to her cousin Julia. She consoled herself with the thought that Mrs Comberton would be very unlikely to attend anything that smelled of the shop.

'What if nobody comes?' Eve asked D'Angers anxiously as the hour of the opening drew near.

'Then we shall have a lot of wine to consume and shall get most horribly drunk,' he told her. 'But some people will come, I am sure.'

By half past three, Eve was pleased to acknowledge that the Frenchman was quite right. A number of ladies, who identified themselves as being previous customers, appeared at about ten past three, and although they made no purchases, they were pleased to renew their subscriptions to the library, and to take a glass of lemonade, which Mrs Castle had thoughtfully prepared for the consumption of those who did not care for wine. Eve also noted with satisfaction that the same ladies were eager to peruse the magazines that were on display. She hoped that this facility would draw her customers back long before they needed to change their books. Once on the premises, who knew what purchases they might make?

The Vicar of St James's appeared with his wife, and wished Eve good fortune with her venture. She had attended church regularly since her arrival in London, and was glad to find that the clergyman recognized her. He expressed his delight that the shop was opening again. 'I shall be coming in to ask you to order theological tomes for me,' he said beaming. Eve smiled back at him, hoping that he could not tell from her expression that she did not have the slightest idea how to do this.

'Mrs Scorer! Your little venture would appear to be a success. My congratulations.'

'Thank you, Mr Harpin,' replied Eve, turning to the newcomer who was accompanied by Monceux as before. Suddenly remembering something that had happened very recently, she said to the Frenchman 'I understand that you were looking for something here the other day. I'm sorry that I was not here to help you. Was it any book in particular?'

The Frenchman flushed. '*Non, non, madame,*' he replied. 'I was not looking for anything at all! Just browsing, I think you say?'

Mrs Castle was summoned to provide wine for the two new arrivals. Appreciative noises were made about the wine, particularly by Monceux, who tasted it with all the air of a connoisseur.

'You must tell me the name of your supplier, *madame*,' he said, by this time having recovered his composure. 'I would not be ashamed to produce such from my very own cellars.'

'*Your* cellars,' hissed D'Angers, who just 'happened' to jog Monceux's elbow in passing. Unfortunately for him, however, the wine spilled not onto Monceux's linen, but onto Eve's gown. '*Tiens, madame!*' he cried, his face turning pale. 'A thousand pardons for my clumsiness.'

'So I should think!' she said sharply, as she hurried past him, excusing herself to the others. 'Save your private scores for your private time if you please.' Anxious not to keep the company waiting, she ran up to her room, first putting her head round the door of the kitchen, where Biddy Todd was washing glasses, and telling her to come upstairs.

'M. D'Angers spilled wine on my gown,' she said to the woman. 'I'll need to change.' Once in her room, she scrambled out of her gown, and eyed the stain with regret. 'I'd like you to sponge this with soda water,' she told Biddy. 'It might just be possible to save it.'

'Very good, ma'am,' answered Biddy in an expressionless voice. 'Would there be anything else?'

'Yes of course there would,' Eve answered, more impatiently than she intended. She seized another of her new gowns almost at random. 'Fasten me into this, would you?'

A sudden thought came into her head as Biddy was fastening the back of her gown. 'Did you ever do this for Mme Lascelles, Biddy?' she asked.

She felt Biddy's fingers stop briefly as if the question had taken her by surprise. 'Only after her maid left sudden, ma'am,' she answered, as she finished her task. 'Would that be all, now?'

'Yes, that's all, thank you.' She paused, remembering what it had been like to be at Julia's beck and call. 'I'm sorry I was impatient,' she began. Then she realized that Biddy had already gone.

It was only when Eve was looking at herself

in the mirror that she noticed that the new gown that she had chosen was cut much lower than the one that Biddy had taken away, and was of a much lighter shade of mauve. It did not make her look at all business-like, she decided regretfully. All the same, it would just have to do. There was no time to change again, and no one upstairs to help her either.

She went downstairs and was pleased to hear the sound of many voices raised in conversation. The opening was going very well. On entering the business area, she could see that M. D'Angers was busy wrapping up someone's purchase, whilst another gentle-man waited with books in his hand.

She went into the shop section of the premises, and found two ladies browsing. One of them was her cousin, dressed in pale pink, with a frivolous bonnet trimmed with nodding feathers. The other was dressed much more plainly.

'You are quite a businesswoman now,' she said coldly. 'This is Miss Pewtress, my companion, by the way.'

'I am so pleased that you were both able to come,' Eve answered, smiling warmly at Miss Pewtress. She did not envy the companion her position.

'No need to ask what kind of customers

you are hoping to attract,' Julia went on, eyeing Eve's neckline.

Not wanting to continue this conversation for fear she might say something uncivil, Eve turned away with a brief 'excuse me.' She noticed that the door to the reading-room was open, and went in to see whether anyone might have gone in there seeking help. No sooner was she inside than the door closed behind her, and to her dismay she found herself face to face with Horace Bunty. He put down a volume that he had been inspecting. His eyes widened appreciatively at the sight of her gown.

'Mrs Scorer! And looking more charming than ever!' he exclaimed.

'Mr Bunty! I see you have discovered our reading-room,' she said, choosing to ignore his remark.

'Why yes, and count myself very fortunate in so doing,' he returned.

'So that you may peruse your volume in privacy?' she suggested, indicating his book. 'In that case, I will leave you to your reading.'

'Now don't run away,' he answered in a caressing tone, as he took a step towards her so that she was forced to walk around the table in order to keep her distance. 'I thought I had made it clear to you how much you attract me.'

'And I thought that I had made it clear at Stonecrop Manor that your attentions were unwelcome,' she responded frankly. 'Why you might suppose that they would be any more welcome to me in London is a mystery to me.'

'My dear, I would follow you to the ends of the earth,' he said, changing his direction, so that she was forced to do the same.

'Pray save yourself the trouble sir,' she said, making a dart for the door. 'And now I must attend to my other customers.'

'Not so fast, madam shopkeeper,' he responded, catching hold of her by the waist. 'This customer is not yet satisfied.'

'Unhand me, sir,' she cried, seizing hold of the book that he had discarded and striking him on the head with it.

'Damnation,' he declared, releasing her. He was about to catch hold of her again, when the door swung open and Colonel Ballantyne appeared, a glass of wine in his hand.

'I beg pardon if I am intruding, ma'am,' he said. His tone was polite, but his expression was cold and disapproving.

'Not at all,' Eve responded, raising her hands to her hair to see if it was disarranged, then dropping them swiftly when she realized how incriminating this would look. 'Mr Bunty had come in here to examine this volume in privacy, and I was just assuring him that he might take it on approval and purchase it later.'

Bunty smirked. 'Mrs Scorer is as obliging as she has always been,' he murmured.

'So it would seem,' Ballantyne replied. 'I do believe your party is a success, ma'am.'

'Yes, it is,' Eve agreed. Then because it would have been unbelievably churlish to say nothing at this point, she added, 'Thank you for the wine. More than one person has remarked upon its quality.'

'*Your* wine,' said Bunty to the colonel, before turning to Eve. 'You told me nothing of this before. We are very obliged to Colonel Ballantyne, are we not, my dear?'

'*I* am certainly obliged to him,' Eve responded, stepping back as if to distance herself from Bunty's possessive remark. 'I fail to see how you should feel similarly indebted.'

'You must allow me to have your best interests at heart,' Bunty responded, raising her hand to his lips before excusing himself and slipping out of the room.

Ballantyne put his glass down on the table and picked up the book that Bunty had been examining. 'Cleland's *Memoirs of a Woman of Pleasure*,' he observed. 'I would hardly have thought that Bunty would need to take that on approval, would you?'

'Despite what you might think, I do not give my stock away to anyone,' Eve retorted, her chin high.

'That wasn't what I meant,' Ballantyne answered mildly. 'My remark was more to do with the fact that he would surely be familiar with this kind of literature.'

'Oh,' responded Eve blushing.

'Incidentally, do you sell and lend literature to anyone who asks for it? Would you be prepared to sell this volume to my cousin, for example?'

'To your cousin?' Eve echoed blankly.

'Oh come now, ma'am! You must surely have given this matter some thought, and if you have not, then you should have done. Cleland's book contains graphic descriptions of the act of love. Would you be prepared to sell such a book to my ward, or to other unmarried girls? What of the other volumes that you sell here? Do you exercise any control over who buys what?'

Eve did not know whether she was more annoyed with Ballantyne for asking such a question, or with herself for not considering such a matter, but she was determined that he should not shout her down. 'I have hardly had a chance to do so,' she retorted. 'The shop has opened for the first time today.'

'And have any of the young women who have been borrowing or buying books laid their hands on items that would not be considered suitable by their parents?'

'This is a shop, and not a nursery,' Eve declared. 'Those parents and guardians who wish to limit their daughters' choice of literature would do well to make sure that their charges are always accompanied.'

'So you are saying, Mrs Scorer, that when Victoria comes here, I should always accompany her,' said the colonel, his voice suddenly losing its hard edge.

'Yes, if you wish to keep a constant watch on her literary tastes. You are obviously the perfect person to guide her, acquainted as you are with the contents of unsuitable books.'

'I'm obliged to you, ma'am. You have provided me with the perfect excuse for calling. As for my own reading matter, I'm not a schoolgirl, I'm a fully grown man.'

They were standing on the same side of the table. Ballantyne put down the book that he was still holding, and took a step closer. With a shock of surprise, Eve looked up into his eyes and realized that he intended to kiss her. A few minutes ago, she had been dodging around the table in order to escape Horace Bunty's unwelcome embrace. This time, she knew that she would not have to run or dodge. The colonel's disability would ensure that it would not be necessary to do such a thing. Nevertheless, she should have been retreating behind the same table now; for some reason she found herself glued to the spot.

Not for the first time, she acknowledged to herself that she found him attractive. He had said that he was a fully grown man. Now, as never before, she was suddenly aware of his potent masculinity. It occurred to her that it would be all too easy to step forward into his arms. Then she noticed the discarded volume out of the corner of her eye. Ballantyne had never really taken back the things that he had said about her. Only a few moments ago, he had suggested that she might be willing to sell unsuitable material to young girls. Was his opinion of her really so low? If so, she had no intention of confirming his error by melting into his embrace like some camp-follower.

'You need no excuse, Colonel,' she said formally, stepping away from him and towards the door. 'Edmund's commanding officer will always be welcome here. Forgive me, I must see to my customers.'

To her relief, no one appeared to be taking any notice of her, or discussing for how long she had been absent. She reflected thankfully that a number of people had seen her gown splashed with wine. No doubt several of them supposed that she had only just returned from changing it. A swift glance around informed her that Mr Bunty was deep in conversation with some of the other guests, and she breathed a sigh of relief. At least he had not been hovering about the door waiting for her return.

Miss Mirfield and Colonel Ballantyne stayed for a flattering length of time, and Eve was left in no doubt that the colonel was the hero of the hour. He remained seated for much of the time, and was very much the centre of attention, gazed at by admiring females who kept asking him about the brave deeds that had caused his injury. He seemed to Eve to be very reticent on this matter, a thing for which she had to give him credit, however reluctantly.

'He is selling out,' Miss Mirfield confided, when no one else was nearby. 'Apparently his leg will never fully recover, and will always be unreliable and cause him pain.'

'What will he do now?'

'At the moment, he seems to occupy himself chiefly by breathing down my neck,' Victoria answered frankly. 'His mama hopes that we will marry, but that will not happen.'

'Really?' Eve responded. The colonel

appeared to be engaged in a flirtation with Julia, who was darting occasional glances about to see who might be watching.

'It must be because I am related to him, but I do not find him attractive *at all*,' declared Miss Mirfield. 'Do you, Mrs Scorer?'

The question took her by surprise. 'Why, I . . . I . . . I had not thought of the matter,' she answered, blushing furiously Her mind immediately flashed back to that moment in the reading-room when she had been very close to allowing him to kiss her. 'That is to say, he is very . . . very striking.'

'I thought you would,' Miss Mirfield replied, matter-of-factly. 'Anyway, he will be obliged to look after his estates in Berkshire eventually,' she went on. 'He inherited them from his uncle on his father's side. The sooner he goes to see them the better as far as I am concerned. Then I can . . . ' She paused, colouring.

'You can . . . ?' Eve prompted.

'I can make friends without reference to him,' Miss Mirfield finished demurely, her eyes cast down. Eve wondered which gentleman had caught her eye this time, and if the colonel was warning him off. Victoria might not find the colonel attractive. It did not necessarily follow that there would be no marriage. Miss Mirfield was undoubtedly a very attractive young lady, and plenty of marriages took place because of family reasons. Furthermore, now that he was seriously wounded and social occasions had become difficult for him, he might prefer to marry someone with whom he was already acquainted and go to his estates as soon as possible.

Eve's limited experience of the colonel led her to believe that if he was set upon a certain course of action, it would be quite difficult to stand in his way. Miss Mirfield might find herself married to the gentleman despite her inclinations. In those circumstances, she reflected, observing Julia's gloved hand on the colonel's arm as she made some point, someone else might well find her nose put out of joint!

16

That evening, Ballantyne ate alone, since his mother and Victoria were engaged to dine with friends then go on to a ball. One of the few advantages that the colonel perceived in indulging in his present deceit was the opportunity that it presented for avoiding social occasions.

He was not a man who enjoyed balls and ridottos and the like. His experience of such gatherings was that people would do their best to put on some kind of false show about their circumstances, appearance, and affections, and would then try to deceive as many others as possible. Pretence of any kind was abhorrent to him; he liked plain dealing and honesty, so even under ordinary circumstances, society parties made him wary and uncomfortable. From the moment when he had undertaken his present commitment for Pitt, he had felt uneasy. His subterfuge, though undertaken for purely patriotic reasons, meant that in his own eyes he was no better than the worst of society butterflies. He was therefore glad of any excuse to absent himself from fashionable gatherings.

He had not realized how embarrassing it would be to go into his club. Only the previous day he had entered White's and bumped into another officer who had been obliged to sell out because he had lost an arm in combat. He had offered his sympathy, and the other man, seeing him walking with a limp, had returned the compliment. Ballantyne had forced himself to receive the other man's good wishes, but inside, he had felt like the worst scoundrel unhung. Consequently, he was thankful to be spending the evening alone at home, free from the obligation to play a part.

He did not mind his own company. He was not a taciturn man, but he had a well-stocked mind, and was happy to spend an evening with a book or the newspaper, or even with his own thoughts.

His thoughts on this occasion were not particularly agreeable however. He could not get out of his mind the image of Mrs Scorer walking towards the tea-room with Max Hadleigh on one side and Horace Bunty hovering close by; nor could he forget the sight of her raising her hands to tidy her hair after Bunty's advances.

Why was he so bothered about Mrs Scorer's true nature? Was it simply to do with his regard for the honour of the regiment? Or was it to do with the way that he felt when he looked at her picture? He had sent the miniature back with regret, and had found, to his great annoyance, that he missed it. Even remembering it seemed to conjure up feelings of yearning; of longing to have a woman waiting at home for him; a woman whose word could be relied upon, who would rather die than betray him and in whom his honour would find a safe haven.

It was as he was musing upon these matters over a glass of port that the doorbell rang, and the butler came in with the welcome tidings that Captain Lord Bradwell had arrived.

'My dear fellow, this is a welcome surprise,' declared the colonel, striding across the room to greet his guest, and in his pleasure quite forgetting that he ought to be limping.

'I'm glad to hear you say so,' answered Bradwell. 'I've just come from my sister's house. I went to pay her a visit, but found that she was on the point of going out. Clearly she didn't know what to do with me, so I decided to come here.'

'Well I'm certainly glad to have you. You save me from my own thoughts, which to be honest aren't that fruitful at the moment. Have you dined?'

Bradwell grinned. 'I'm devilish sharp set, if

you would like to know.'

'Then sit down and I'll ring for something. I take it you'd rather eat in here than in state in the dining room?' Ballantyne crossed to the fireplace and rang the bell.

'Far rather. I see your leg's recovered.'

The colonel glanced down ruefully. 'Damn. Now I'll have to tell you the whole story, but not until we're sure of being alone.'

The captain's needs were made known, and in no time he was tucking into a large portion of the steak pie that had been served at dinner, washed down with an excellent red wine, followed by a portion of a rich almond pudding known as a hedgehog.

'That's better, b'Gad,' he declared when his plate was empty. 'I wasn't sorry to have missed dinner at m'sister-in-law's. She does tend to see things from her own point of view. Just now, Bunty almost appears to have taken up residence and I don't like the man.'

Once the plates were taken away, the two men sat in front of the fire sharing a bottle of port.

'I thought you were fixed in Derbyshire for the time being,' the colonel remarked, after an easy silence.

'That had been my intention,' Bradwell agreed. 'M'father doesn't seem to have a lot of time for me at present. He's got himself occupied with reorganizing the local militia. He's convinced that the present peace won't last and he wants to do his bit to defeat Napoleon. You should hear him ranting about Boney, striding up and down, haranguing the servants about being on the alert! He's taught all the male indoor servants to shoot, and he's now beginning on the females!'

'Good grief!' breathed Ballantyne. 'You don't say.'

'Oh, I'm quite serious. I was present when he had them all lined up, and there was little Jenny, the upstairs maid, with a rifle almost as big as she was in her hands. 'Come on, m'lass, no need to be afraid', Father was saying, while Higgins, the footman, was showing off because he'd managed to catch the edge of the target. Then Jenny raises the rifle and shoots the target square in the middle, better than anyone! Father'd forgotten she was one of Farmer Clay's daughters, and he one of the best shots in the county!'

Ballantyne laughed. 'You didn't want to stay and help him, then?'

'Wasn't needed, old fellow. Decided I'd come to town and look up a few friends.'

'I'm flattered that you sought me out first.'

'So tell me about your leg. I gather there's a bit of a mystery attached to it.'

'By all means,' Ballantyne replied, lowering his voice. 'But before I do, would you mind just glancing outside the door?'

Bradwell raised his brows, but did as he was asked, saying 'No one there', as he came back to his place.

Ballantyne refilled their glasses. 'Perhaps you recall that the reason why I was unable to accompany you to London originally was because I was summoned elsewhere on business.'

'I recall.'

'I was summoned by Pitt,' Ballantyne explained, and he then went on to tell the other man what had occurred. 'So you see, as far as the world is concerned, I am still suffering from the effects of my injury. It was only my surprise at seeing you that made me forget myself.'

'No one will learn the truth from me,' Bradwell assured him. 'And, since you came back on my ship, I shall be in the perfect position to confirm your story. How are things going? Have you found out anything new? Any Frenchies sneaking about?'

Ballantyne shook his head. 'Everything appears to be as it should be,' he answered. He paused. 'There's one coincidence that might interest you: Mrs Scorer, about whom we spoke onboard ship — '

'The notorious widow?' Bradwell interjected.

'The same lady,' Ballantyne agreed, surprised at the irritation he felt at Bradwell's description. 'Anyway, Mrs Scorer is the proprietor of the shop in question.' Again he paused. 'She does not appear to be quite as you described her.'

'Not I,' answered Bradwell, his hands raised. 'I've never met her. It was Julia who did the describing. So what's your next step?'

'Oh, I'll continue to keep an eye on the place. I've a suspicion the French haven't finished with it yet.'

'If you want any help, just let me know. I'm not needed back on my ship for a while yet.'

Ballantyne thanked him, then for a while the conversation turned to other matters, notably any mutual acquaintances who were to be found in London at this time.

'I have met the fellow you were referring to earlier; Horace Bunty who, I think, is a neighbour of yours in Derbyshire,' said Ballantyne.

Bradwell nodded. 'The family's known to m'father. 'Decent lot', he said to me, 'but that Horace Bunty is a bad hat. Any family you know with females, make sure they're well-protected. No woman's safe with him'.'

'Indeed?' enquired Ballantyne in an arrested tone.

'Oh yes. M'father may be a mad old duffer in some ways, but he has his finger on the pulse of what's going on in the district all right. You've got a young cousin, haven't you?'

'Yes. She's my ward.'

'Well, keep her out of his way. Not that she would be at much risk with you at her back. Apparently it's widows, governesses, companions, *you* know; the kind of woman without a man to offer protection; that's the sort he targets.'

Bradwell stayed for perhaps another hour, then left, having taken a room in a hotel. 'Wouldn't stay with Julia for any price,' he said frankly. 'The woman talks too much, and it's most of it nonsense. She's a terrible flirt as well; or hadn't you noticed?'

After he had gone, Ballantyne sat thinking about Mrs Scorer. The evidence against her good character which had at one time seemed to him to be so compelling, now appeared to be on the flimsy side. The errors that she herself had made in London could have been committed by any woman trying to manage on her own in the capital for the first time. The chief complaints against her came from Julia Comberton, a woman who, by her own brother-in-law's evidence, talked too much nonsense, and saw things only from her own point of view. Horace Bunty was now revealed to be a scoundrel. The more he thought about it, the more he became convinced that Eve Scorer really was the brave, honourable woman about whom her late husband had spoken with such pride. If so, then he, Ballantyne, must visit her as soon as possible and put matters right.

17

'Now is this not fortuitous?' said a familiar but most unwelcome voice.

Eve spun round to see Horace Bunty standing in the entrance to the rear of the premises that constituted the shop. M. D'Angers was not present as his mother had been taken ill that day. Miss Sparrow had gone with Luke for a walk. Mrs Castle and Biddy Todd were both in the kitchen. There was no one within call. Suddenly, she felt very vulnerable.

'I had supposed that in London, it would be much harder to find you alone,' he went on in a conversational tone, 'but I find that the reverse is the case.'

'I wish you would manage to accept the fact that I have no desire for your company and your attentions,' Eve told him, wishing that he were not between her and the only way out.

'Now you know you don't really mean that,' he replied.

'Of course I really mean it. Why would I say it otherwise?'

'Because you want to fan the flames of my

261

passion.' They were both so absorbed with what was being said that neither of them noticed the sound of the shop door opening. 'Believe me, my love, the more you struggle, the more you protest, the more my desire for you grows. When I held you in my arms at Stonecrop Manor — '

' — You mean, when you forced yourself upon me,' Eve interrupted swiftly.

'As you wish. It matters little. The fact of the matter is that your struggles inflamed me, and the memory of them inflames me still.' He stepped forward and grasped her by the arms.

Eve pulled against him and, as on that previous occasion in her cousin's house, realized with alarm how strong he was. If he chose to force himself upon her now, there was not a thing she could do to prevent him. 'Upon my soul, what do I have to do to make you understand that your unwanted attentions revolt me?'

'All you have to do, ma'am, is inform *me* of the fact. I shall make sure that you are not troubled again.'

Bunty swung round to see Colonel Ballantyne standing in the entrance, His stance was deceptively casual. Only by his fists, half-clenched by his sides, could it be seen that he was ready for action.

'This lady and I have an understanding,' said Bunty. 'It is purely between the two of us.'

'Is it really?' replied Ballantyne limping slightly, as he passed Bunty in order to stand next to Eve. 'You see, from what I heard just now, it appeared to me that you and Mrs Scorer understand very different things. You seem to think that you can force yourself on a lady who has refused your attentions, whereas Mrs Scorer thinks that you are an obnoxious worm who ought to be ejected forthwith.' He paused. 'Speaking personally, I'm rather inclined to the lady's point of view.'

'This is none of your business, Ballantyne,' snarled Bunty.

'On the contrary,' Ballantyne replied. 'Mrs Scorer's husband was an officer in my regiment, and in his absence it is therefore my right and my duty to protect her. Do you go through that door of your own volition, or do I throw you out of it?' His tone hardened and any pretence of casual, social conversation disappeared. 'Please don't imagine that because of my injury I cannot do what I threaten. I can assure you that I am quite capable of giving you the thrashing you deserve, and by God, I feel more inclined to do so with every minute that you stand there.'

Bunty prudently took a step back towards

the entrance. 'Under your protection, is she?' he sneered. 'I might have guessed. I'll see myself out, ma'am. No wonder you don't want my embraces. You're already being well satisfied elsewhere.'

Ballantyne took a step towards him, but he turned on his heel and swiftly left the shop.

The colonel turned to Eve. 'Do you want me to call him to account?' he asked.

'No, no,' she answered, more shaken than she had expected. 'But I would like to sit down.' She made her way into the book-room, followed by Ballantyne, and sat down at the table.

'Would you like something to drink?' he asked her. She shook her head. He pulled out the chair next to her and sat down. 'Have you had many such unpleasant scenes to deal with?' He was thinking of the time that she had been in London, but Eve misunderstood him.

'Ever since I came to live with Julia,' she replied in a low voice. 'He does not seem to be able to take no for an answer.'

'Was there no one to help you?' the colonel asked, taking her hand.

She shook her head. 'Not really. Julia has her own reasons for wanting to have him around, and I had Luke's security to consider. Greet, the butler, was very good, and Lavinia helped me when she could. Most of the time, I managed to keep out of his way, but because he lived so close, he used to turn up unannounced. Once he came upon me in the garden . . . ' She paused. 'You cannot think how often I used to wish that Edmund was there to protect me.'

As he sat holding her hand, he felt a drop of moisture fall onto his, and he realized that she was crying. Without hesitation, he gave a gentle tug and pulled her into his arms. For him, at that moment, all doubts were resolved. This was where he wanted her to be; in his arms. This was the woman that he wanted for his wife; to be what the regiment would call the colonel's lady.

She did not shed many tears. Presently, she said in a low voice, 'What made you come to my rescue just now? You have not always had a very high opinion of me, I think.'

'I have not always had a very accurate idea of you,' he answered frankly. 'I was misled by some of the foolish things that you did, and by comments from your cousin and from Bunty himself. I should have relied more upon the description that I received from your husband.'

'I'm sure he painted a rosy picture of me,' Eve said.

'I am very sure he did not,' Ballantyne

answered, quite forgetting that he had been of that opinion earlier. 'But understand this, ma'am: I meant what I said when I spoke to Bunty just now. You are under my care. Never again will you have to face a rake such as he without knowing that you have me at your back.'

She smiled up at him. He bent his head and she knew that he was about to kiss her. Edmund Scorer had been her first and only love. Certainly, she had never before wanted any other man to kiss her, but at this moment, she knew that she very much wanted to be kissed by Jason Ballantyne. She also knew that for all his high-handed behaviour and masterful ways, she had but to say one word and he would draw back. She didn't say it, but instead, raised one hand to touch his cheek. His lips met hers, briefly, before drawing away then closing upon hers again in a long, searching kiss that made her toes curl up and seemed to ignite a fire in the pit of her stomach at one and the same time.

The kiss ended; after how long, she could not have said. It might have lasted minutes or hours, because time had seemed to stand still. When at last he drew back, he looked at her for a long moment before saying 'Eve — '

Before he could complete his sentence, the door opened and Mrs Castle came in. 'There now, ma'am, I felt sure when I saw that Bunty leaving with a face like thunder that he had been up to mischief and that you'd sent him packing with a flea in his ear. And now here's the colonel, all ready to cheer you up. Shall I bring some wine, ma'am?'

'Thank you, Mrs Castle, I refused some earlier, but I think I would like some now. Will you stay, Colonel?'

Ballantyne, who had stood up at once when Mrs Castle had come in, shook his head, his manner rather stiff and formal. 'No thank you, ma'am. I believe I must be going. For the time being, may I suggest that you are never completely alone in the shop? Bunty is not the only rake in London, and it is unwise not to have another person within call.' He bowed, and left.

That night, Eve lay awake for a long time, thinking about what had occurred. She knew that given her circumstances in Derbyshire, some ladies would have succumbed to Horace Bunty's advances. This was not something that she had ever felt the smallest desire to do. She would never want to do anything that could cause Luke to feel ashamed of his mama in the future. She had known that Bunty was attracted by her, but she had never suspected that he would pursue her to London. She had thought that she would have to fight him alone. This afternoon, Colonel Ballantyne had made it clear that he constituted himself as her champion.

He had begun by thinking badly of her. Something had happened to change his opinion, and she was glad of it. But it was not enough. When he had taken her in his arms and kissed her, she had realized that she wanted much more of him, but she was very unsure of her motives. She had had to fend for herself for a long time. The idea of placing her burdens upon the shoulders of another was very tempting — especially when they were such broad shoulders. What was more, the idea of succumbing to the colonel's embrace did not repel her by any means. On the contrary . . .

But Colonel Ballantyne did not deserve to be made use of in such a way, she told herself firmly. In any case, she could not be sure that he wanted to offer her more than what his duty required, despite that kiss, the memory of which caused a shiver to run up her spine, even now.

Then there was Luke to be considered. Bunty was right when he said that many men would not want to take on another man's child. But Eve was determined that she would never marry again unless the man who asked her was prepared to be a father to Luke.

She turned over and took herself to task. Why was she thinking in this way? Just because a sizzle of attraction had sparked between herself and Ballantyne, it did not mean that any more could come of it. She closed her eyes and determinedly gave her mind to consideration of new clothes for Luke for the summer, and in no time, she was asleep.

The following morning brought an invitation from Mrs Ballantyne to Mrs Scorer and Miss Sparrow to dine in Berkeley Square that evening. After consultation with Miss Sparrow, and with Mrs Castle to make sure that the latter would be able to look after Luke, Eve sent off an acceptance, and then set about choosing a gown from amongst her new acquisitions. That evening, however, as she was getting ready, Miss Sparrow came in, looking a little pale. 'I have a headache, and really do not feel well enough to go out,' she said. 'What is to be done? You cannot go alone.'

'Of course I can,' Eve replied bracingly. 'If Goodman summons a hackney for me I shall be safe enough. I am a widow after all.'

'But it is not fitting,' answered Miss Sparrow. 'Perhaps I could go with you in the hackney and then come straight home afterwards?'

'I would not dream of being so cruel,' Eve replied. 'I told you, I shall be perfectly safe. I am only travelling from door to door after all.'

On her arrival in Berkeley Square, Colonel Ballantyne met her in the hall on his way to the drawing room. He was dressed in dark evening clothes, the severity of their cut doing nothing to hide his muscular physique and, to Eve's eyes, he looked immaculate, imposing and very masculine. She was glad that she had chosen to wear a new gown in silver grey, with a high waistline, puff sleeves and a modest *décolletage*.

Ballantyne was regretful when he heard that Miss Sparrow was detained, but he was visibly annoyed on hearing that Eve had come on her own in a common hackney. 'A message would have brought my carriage to collect you,' he told her. 'I am exceedingly embarrassed that any guest of mine should have had to travel in such a way.'

'I would have been very late if I had waited to send a message,' Eve told him. 'In any case, I sent Goodman to summon a hackney for me, and told him to be certain that he found a very respectable man. I am hoping that you will perform the same service for me at the end of the evening.'

The colonel made a sound very like a

snort. 'You will go home under my escort,' he said decisively.

Eve laughed. 'You make it sound as though you will be arresting me,' she said.

'Believe me, ma'am, I am quite capable of so doing if you do not respect my wishes.'

'In that case, I had better put myself in your hands,' Eve replied, then coloured because of how the words might sound.

Ballantyne inclined his head politely, taking her hand and raising it to his lips. 'I cannot think of anything more desirable,' he remarked. Her hand looked very small, clasped in his strong, brown one. Immediately, she remembered how he had taken her in his arms, the kiss that they had shared, and her thoughts of the previous night. Could it be that he really was seriously attracted to her? She was glad that he ushered her into the drawing room immediately after this. Her thoughts were far too disturbing for her to dwell on them at such a time.

Mrs Ballantyne and Miss Mirfield were both waiting in the drawing room, and when she saw how fashionably attired they were, Eve was glad that she had taken trouble with her dress. Mrs Ballantyne rose from her seat to greet her visitor, but she looked as if the effort was almost too much for her. Her welcome was very gracious, conveying the impression that she was conferring a singular honour upon the visitor.

Miss Mirfield, who looked charming in a gown of palest blue trimmed with silver lace, greeted Eve with the utmost friendliness. 'I am so pleased that you have been able to come,' she said. 'Are you here alone, though, dear Mrs Scorer?'

'I fear so,' Eve replied. 'Lavinia sends her regrets. She has a nasty headache.'

'That is most unfortunate,' Mrs Ballantyne murmured. 'Some of us, of course, have to live with our ill health. I declare, if I were to give up my engagements every time I was ill, I should never go anywhere or do anything.'

'That would be a sad loss to the fashionable world, Mama,' observed the colonel. 'Mrs Scorer, you must allow me to introduce you to Lord Bradwell; that is, if you have not already met.'

The only remaining occupant of the room came forward, bowing politely. He was a bronzed, fair-haired gentleman, not as tall as Ballantyne, but strongly built, with broad shoulders, and a lean, athletic figure, well in proportion. Eve had never met him before, but she had come across the Earl of Wirksworth and thought that she could detect a likeness.

Bradwell smiled politely. 'No, Mrs Scorer

and I haven't met, but I think you know my father, ma'am.'

'Yes indeed, I have met Lord Wirksworth,' Eve replied. 'You have a look of him, Lord Bradwell. Your nephew, Thomas, bears some resemblance to you as well.'

'It's the Comberton nose,' answered his lordship. 'We can't escape the damn — I mean dashed — thing!'

Dinner, which was announced soon after Eve's arrival, was well served with carefully chosen wines, and the table around which they gathered was not too large for their party. 'There is a larger dining room, but we would all have looked rather absurd sitting in there,' Ballantyne explained.

'We must use it more, now that you are finished with the army,' said Mrs Ballantyne. 'At last I shall be able to entertain with a host available more frequently.'

'Yes, Mama,' answered the colonel, looking down at his plate.

Eve's heart swelled with pity for him. How could his mother be so insensitive? 'How did you and Lord Bradwell meet?' she asked him quickly. 'I thought that the army and the navy were at loggerheads.'

'Naturally we are,' Bradwell answered with a twinkle. 'The truth, of course, is that the navy is superior and the army know it. That is what they find so difficult.'

'I would very much like to know how you manage to come to that conclusion,' remarked the colonel.

'My dear fellow, it's obvious,' answered Bradwell. 'Without us to transport you, you'd never be able to get to anywhere in order to fight your battles.'

'Whereas without us, you sailors would simply float round and round with nothing to do and nowhere to go.'

Eve watched the two men as they exchanged banter. Hitherto she had thought that the colonel was a good-humoured if rather serious man; now, she saw that that need not be the case.

'For my part, I think that the army uniforms are much prettier,' declared Miss Mirfield, directing a sideways glance at Lord Bradwell that made Eve sit up and take notice.

'Prettier, eh?' echoed Bradwell, wrinkling his brow as he looked at Ballantyne. 'I've thought of Jason as being many things, but I'll confess that pretty was not one of them.'

'Oh, my dear son,' murmured Mrs Ballantyne. 'How splendid you looked in your red and gold! How sad it is to see you thus!'

'Trust you to dampen my pretensions, Mama,' the colonel said humorously. 'I suppose you'll say that I don't even look pretty any more!'

Not for the first time, Eve felt a strong desire to give Mrs Ballantyne a good shake. She did not seem to have the smallest idea of how insensitive she was being towards her son, who must surely feel a terrible sense of loss at the ending of his military career. The silly woman really ought to decide what it was she wanted. At one minute, she had been rejoicing that she would have a host on the spot. At the next, she was complaining because Ballantyne was not in his regimentals.

'I dare say *my* son would say that you did if he thought that it would please you,' Eve remarked.

'How old is your son, ma'am?' Bradwell asked. 'Is he in London with you?'

'Of course,' Eve responded. 'I could never think of leaving him behind. He is six years old, Lord Bradwell.'

The discussion then turned away from military matters and did not touch them again before the ladies left the gentlemen to their port.

'So that's Mrs Scorer,' Bradwell said, after the door had closed behind the ladies, and the two men had taken their seats again. Ballantyne merely responded with a grunt.

'She's not how I imagined her to be,' the captain went on.

'In what way?' Ballantyne asked, his chin up, a hint of challenge in his voice.

'Steady on,' replied the captain, one hand raised. 'No disrespect intended — quite the reverse, in fact.' He paused. 'I liked the way that she spoke about her son. Julia's left Thomas behind at Stonecrop Manor.'

'Yes, I know,' Ballantyne replied. He was remembering how he had overheard Mrs Comberton telling Victoria what a nuisance children were.

'To be honest, I suspect I've been getting a rather inaccurate view of things from my sister-in-law,' Bradwell confessed. 'But she's the only one who ever writes to me, y'see.'

Ballantyne nodded. 'I know what it's like to yearn for news from home,' he said. 'My mother writes. Victoria's a more lively correspondent, even though she does often ask me for things.'

'Things?'

'Ponies, gowns, larger allowances, that sort of thing, but she does write an interesting letter.'

'Intelligent girl,' agreed the captain. Then after a moment or two he added, 'D'you think she would write to me — with your permission, of course?'

Ballantyne grinned. 'Ask her,' he said. He knew that his mother would have no objection. To have Victoria in touch with the heir to the Earl of Wirksworth would be a coup indeed!

At the close of the evening, Colonel Ballantyne announced his intention of escorting Eve home in his carriage.

'No need, m'dear fellow,' declared Bradwell. 'I'll go with Mrs Scorer with the greatest of pleasure.'

'But did you not say that you had an engagement that would take you to the other end of town?' asked the colonel, his brows raised.

'No, I . . . ' the captain began. Then, his brow clearing he went on, 'Of course, I had forgotten. It would be very remiss of me to fail to appear.'

The colonel turned to Eve. 'I promise to behave with perfect propriety,' he told her.

'Of course he will,' murmured Mrs Ballantyne, as Eve made her farewells, thanking her hostess sincerely for what had truly been a very pleasant evening. 'My son has always been the soul of propriety.'

'She makes me sound like a complete stick-in-the-mud,' Ballantyne complained as he climbed after Eve into the carriage that had been summoned for them.

'She is simply proud of her son,' Eve responded. 'Are you an only child, sir?'

Ballantyne nodded. 'I have always been something of a disappointment to her, I fear.'

'A disappointment?' exclaimed Eve disbelievingly. 'But surely she is proud of your achievements in the army?'

'That is the public face that she puts upon it,' he agreed. 'She was always against my going into the army, however. My father, who passed away shortly after I joined his old regiment, was inclined to encourage me. Mama would prefer me to cut a dash in society and squire her to dinners, theatres and balls.'

'She would prefer you to be a Bond Street beau rather than do your duty for your country?'

'She would,' Ballantyne agreed. 'Practically the only thing that she ever saw to recommend my chosen career was my red coat.'

'She must be glad to have you around now,' Eve remarked. She stopped abruptly, recalling the reason for his presence in London. What would balls be like for him now? Even other social occasions, involving staying on one's feet for long periods of time, would be torture. 'I do beg your pardon,' she said, leaning towards him. 'You must think me very insensitive.'

'I do not think you anything of the kind, Mrs Scorer. In fact, there is something I — ' He broke off abruptly, never more annoyed about his subterfuge than at this moment. He had never relished the idea of finding information for Pitt whilst pretending to be more severely injured than he really was. He had agreed to the deceit for the sake of his country, but he had not bargained for meeting the one lady with whom he wanted to be honest and straightforward from the beginning. Her every sympathetic word and gesture made him want to cringe. How would she feel when she realized that all of her sympathy had been squandered upon a man who had nothing wrong with him? Yet although he longed to tell her the truth about himself, he could not do so without Pitt's expressed permission. His training was too strong.

'There is something . . . ?' Eve prompted him.

'Oh, nothing,' he answered. 'Although . . . ' He paused, then went on in an altered tone, 'Mrs Scorer, there is something I must confess to you. It is a deceit that I have practised, and that I must put right.'

'Yes, Colonel?'

'You remember the miniature of you that I returned.'

'Yes, I recall.'

'I did not keep it because it had become damaged.'

'Sir?'

'I kept it by me because I liked to look at it,' he confessed, colouring in the darkness.

'Oh.'

'You don't ask me why. Well I'll tell you anyway. Edmund Scorer was always praising you to the skies; holding you up as a model of love and honour and faithfulness. I'd had some experience of seeing how some army wives behaved when their husbands were out of sight, but because I had such respect for Edmund, I felt sure that you must be different.

'After Edmund was killed, I gathered together all his belongings in order to return them to you. Among them was your miniature. Instead of putting it away with the rest of his things, I kept it for myself, so that I could look at it. God, I must sound like such a fool!' He ran one hand through his hair and turned to look out of the window.

'No,' Eve replied gently. 'No, you don't. You had a great deal of responsibility, I expect. No doubt my picture helped you to forget.'

'Yes, I think it did, for a while,' he agreed. 'Gradually, I started to think that . . . ' He paused. 'Would you think me mad if I said that I began to talk to you?'

'No,' she replied. 'I talked to Edmund's picture every night. I still did so after he died, for a time.'

'Why did you never follow the drum?' he asked her. 'You would have made such a splendid officer's wife in such circumstances.'

She smiled. 'I would have liked to have done so, but it was never possible. Both of Edmund's parents were frail and old, and then there was Luke to think about.' She paused. 'Please do not mistake me, but sometimes it was very tedious at home.'

He recalled Miss Sparrow speaking about the courage of army wives who contrived to manage far from their husbands. 'A military campaign can be tedious at times,' he acknowledged. 'Especially if one is waiting for orders or for some piece of action. Your presence would have enlivened things.'

'Enlivened them?'

'Why certainly. The presence of ladies at the dinner table always raises the men's spirits. I've often observed it.' He paused. 'In your case, however, the excitement generated might have been a little too great for comfort.'

'You are teasing me, I think,' she said cautiously.

'Not at all,' he assured her. Again he paused, not sure whether or not to continue. Eventually he spoke again. 'It is bound to cause something of a stir when one officer falls in love with the wife of another.' His tone was unmistakably sincere.

There was a long silence. Eve could feel her heart beating with slow heavy strokes. He caught hold of her hand. She did not resist, but he could feel her trembling. At length he spoke again. 'There are things about which I cannot be entirely candid at present, and about those I must ask you to trust me. Believe me, when I am free to speak, I will ask you a question, and hope that despite the way I have blundered and hurt your feelings, you might grant me a favourable answer.'

'Colonel Ballantyne, I — '

'Jason.'

'Jason, I hardly know what to say. I have a very real regard for you. I believe I told you that Edmund worshipped you as a hero and encouraged me to do the same. Your injury only makes me honour you the more. Your misunderstanding of my character hurt me deeply, but it could not prevent me from feeling a growing attraction towards you.' She paused, then took a deep breath. 'I could never marry again unless I was sure that my future husband would love Luke as his own.'

'Believe me, I would do so.'

'I do believe you. The other thing that I must say is this.' She paused, then continued resolutely. 'I found pleasure in being married, and have had enough contact with you to know that with you the . . . the intimacies of marriage would hardly be a punishment. But Jason, it would not be fair to marry you unless I was sure that there was more to my regard for you than that.'

'So we are even,' he replied. 'I cannot yet ask you, and you cannot yet answer.' He bent over her in the darkness, caught hold of her chin with his left hand then kissed her on her mouth. It was a brief salute from which he drew back, before kissing her again at greater length, moving his mouth across hers in a way which she found quite intoxicating. She leaned into his embrace, reaching up to stroke the back of his neck where those dark curls grew so profusely. They had only kissed once before, yet the feel of him was becoming familiar to her already, almost like coming home. Whilst part of her was surrendering to the pleasure of his kiss, a section of her brain was thinking, if he keeps doing this, how will I ever be able to refuse him?

They were now turning into Clerkenwell Green. The carriage drew up, and Ballantyne got down carefully, then assisted Eve to alight. 'Do you have your key or shall I ring the bell?'

'I have my key,' Eve said. The colonel put out his hand authoritatively and Eve searched in her reticule for several minutes before saying, 'I thought I had it. I went to see if Lavinia was all right just before I left, and I must have forgotten it.'

'I'll ring,' he said, walking to the front door.

At the same time, Eve pushed at the door which led into the shop. 'It's open.'

Before she could go in, he came to stand behind her, moving more quickly than she would have expected. He grasped her shoulders while she still had her back to him. 'Should anyone have been in here?' he asked in an undertone. As he was speaking, Eve became aware of the smell of recently extinguished candles. She shook her head. Jason pulled her out of the doorway none too gently, thrust her towards the carriage, and entered the shop, crouching down. Eve waited, unsure what to do next.

'Housebreakers I 'spect, ma'am,' said the coachman in a loud whisper. From within there came the sound of something falling, then a shout, the loud report of a pistol, and the noise of footsteps. A muffled figure came out, and darted past Eve, heading towards the city. Moments later, Ballantyne also appeared in the doorway.

'Which way?' he rapped out. Eve pointed and he set off at a run.

'Colonel's leg seems better, don't it?' said the coachman. 'Cor, can't he go?'

'Just what I was thinking myself,' replied Eve grimly.

18

Eve went inside. She would have a word or two to say to Colonel Ballantyne, and for that she did not require an audience. She walked over towards the mantelpiece where she knew that candles were kept. As she did so, she nearly fell over one of the chairs that had somehow become overturned. That must have been the cause of the crash that she had heard, she decided.

It was only as she was lighting the candles that she recalled the coachman speculating that there might have been housebreakers inside. Housebreakers, she thought to herself, realizing that the word was a plural, and that only one intruder had left the premises. Then, as she turned, all thoughts of who might still be present went out of her head as she saw the havoc that had been wrought in her once tidy bookshop. The chair was not the only thing that had been overturned. It looked as if someone had made a strenuous effort to pull all the books off the bookcases, and throw them about the room. In fact, more books were on the floor than remained on the shelves. One of the small tables had been overturned, and a picture had been pulled off the wall.

Eve stood staring about her, unable to take in what had happened. She was brought back to herself by the sound of groaning from the room beyond. Hurrying through, she found what looked at first to be a heap of rags on the floor, but which turned out to be Biddy Todd.

'Biddy!' she exclaimed, kneeling down next to the servant. 'What happened? Were you attacked?'

'I don't rightly know, ma'am,' Biddy murmured, sounding dazed. 'I thought I heard something in here, so I came to have a look. Before I could see anything or do anything, someone struck me down.'

At that moment, the door from the shop into the living quarters opened and Mrs Castle came in wearing her dressing gown. Her honest face wore an anxious expression. 'Oh, my goodness, ma'am,' she exclaimed. 'What has happened here?'

'I don't know, Mrs Castle,' Eve replied, 'It looks very much as though we have had housebreakers.'

'I woke to a terrible sound, miss,' said Mrs Castle. 'Was that a gun, do you think?'

'I'm afraid it was,' Eve answered with a shiver. 'Whoever they were, they must have been desperate fellows. I don't suppose you got a proper look at them, Biddy?'

Biddy shook her head, then winced at the pain caused by the unconsidered movement. 'It all happened too quick. I think he was muffled up. I did hear him shout something out, though.'

'What did he say?' Eve asked her.

'I don't rightly know, ma'am. It didn't sound like English to me.'

'Well you had better get to bed and get some rest,' said Eve. 'Where were Goodman and Todd while all this was going on, by the way?'

'Tim sleeps like a stone,' said Biddy. 'I don't know where Goodman is; I think he might have gone out.'

'I'll get her to bed, ma'am,' said Mrs Castle, helping the other woman to her feet. 'It'll give me something to do.'

'Thank you,' Eve responded. 'I will remain here. I need to have a word with Colonel Ballantyne.' She was conscious of her tone changing as she said his name. She was surprised that she managed to resist actually grinding her teeth.

It was not long before the colonel reappeared. By that time, Eve was alone in the shop, having lit more candles. She had inspected the premises, and found that the library had fared worse than the shop, no doubt because the library was the first section to be encountered by anyone entering the front door. The bookshop itself was comparatively untouched, she was thankful to see. It would have been difficult to sell books that had been damaged by some thief's careless handling.

When the colonel returned, Eve was standing in the library area straightening the pages of a book that had landed on the floor face down.

'I lost him,' said the colonel, leaning against the door post.

'That is not all you have lost, sir,' Eve replied. 'Your limp would appear to have gone. Congratulations.'

He straightened. 'Mrs Scorer, I — ' He broke off, looking round. 'Good God, what has happened here?' he exclaimed, taking a hasty step or two inside the shop.

Had he not moved, she might possibly have been diverted from the main cause of her grievance, but the sight of his powerful, athletic figure moving with ease and confidence kindled her anger afresh.

'You might well ask,' she said, drawing her hand back and slapping him across the face with the full force of her arm.

Big man though he was, he rocked back on

his heels, momentarily caught off balance. 'What the . . . ?'

'How dare you?' she demanded, her voice shaking with fury. 'How dare you masquerade as some kind of war hero, when there is nothing the matter with you?'

'Mrs Scorer . . . Eve . . . ' Again he destroyed his case before he had a chance to make it by stepping forward.

'Encouraging my sympathy!' she stormed, mimicking savagely: ' 'I shall probably never ride again! Whatever will I do now I have to leave the army?' Which leg was it then? Was it this one? Or possibly that one?' So saying she closed swiftly upon him and kicked him first upon one leg then upon the other. He stepped back, holding out a hand to ward her off, whereupon she struck out at that as well.

'That's enough,' he said firmly. 'There is an explanation — '

'Oh, I'm sure there is,' Eve answered sarcastically. 'Are you so inept socially that you need a dash of pity to make your clumsy manners acceptable? Or did you simply want to make game of me? And *you* accused *me* of having a bad character! Oh, why don't you just . . . just go to blazes, Colonel Ballantyne?'

He straightened and stepped back. 'I can see you are in no mood to listen to me tonight,' he began.

'Or at any other time,' she put in swiftly. 'Kindly close the door as you leave.'

'You are mistaken,' he replied. 'I will return when you are cooler. In the meantime, have Goodman secure this door, and make sure that he checks any other entrances. There is more at stake here than you may imagine.'

'Yes sir!' she retorted, straightening and executing an insolent salute.

He made as if to leave, then turned in the doorway. 'By the way, if you were under my command you'd be disciplined for that. It was damned sloppy.'

'And so are you damned sloppy!' she declared, picking up one of the books that had been cast on the table and hurling it at the door, before sitting down at the table and bursting into tears.

The door into the living quarters opened and Mrs Castle appeared. 'I've just given Biddy a sleeping draught — ' she began. Then seeing that Eve was crying, she came hurrying forward. 'O my dear, there now!' she said, as she put an arm around the drooping figure of her mistress.

'Oh Mrs Castle, it's all spoiled!' Eve sobbed. Though whether she meant the damage done to the shop or her relationship with the colonel, which had now been destroyed through his perfidy, she would have been hard put to it to say.

★   ★   ★

Thanks to the sleeping draught which Mrs Castle pressed upon her, Eve had a restful night's sleep and woke, if not feeling very optimistic, at least better equipped to face the challenges of the day. Mrs Castle had stayed up the previous night to make sure that Goodman obeyed the colonel's instructions when he returned, leaving Eve free to retire.

Her thoughts before she succumbed to the draught were not pleasant, and were all centred upon the way in which the colonel had deceived her. He had not confined his deceitful behaviour to her, either, she concluded. Both Goodman and Mrs Castle believed him to be the soul of honour. Even Mrs Ballantyne and Miss Mirfield thought that his injuries were real.

The fact that she was not the only gullible fool soothed her vanity a little, but did nothing to mend her damaged heart, she was forced to admit. She felt even more foolish when she recalled how she had honoured him for his injury and told him so. What a hypocrite he was! She was still composing cutting things to say to him when he returned, which, she told herself, she devoutly hoped that he would not do, when she drifted off to sleep.

She was a little soothed by Miss Sparrow's reaction when they met at the breakfast-table. 'Such a shocking thing!' her companion exclaimed. 'How dreadful for you to find your shop turned upside down!'

'It was even worse for poor Biddy,' Eve pointed out. 'She was struck down by one of the intruders.'

'You think that there was more than one?' asked Miss Sparrow curiously.

'I only saw one person,' Eve answered. 'That does not mean to say that another one had not been present at some point during the proceedings. There was rather a lot of mess for one person to make. I cannot understand why anyone would want to break into a bookshop. Who would want to steal books?'

'Did no one give chase?' Miss Sparrow enquired.

'Colonel Ballantyne — ' Eve said, then stopped. Heaven knew, such a deceitful man deserved to have his lies exposed to the world, but her feelings were still too raw for her to be the one to do it.

'Ah yes, poor man,' murmured the other lady. 'How distressing for him not to be able to catch the miscreants as he would have liked to have done.'

'Most distressing,' Eve agreed, suddenly finding herself wanting to talk through her teeth again. She went to her room and spent a little time making adjustments to her appearance. She knew that she was only putting off the awful moment, but she really did not want to see the havoc that her intruder had wrought. It had looked bad enough by candlelight; by the cruel light of day it would surely look much worse.

She went slowly down the stairs and opened the door which led into the library. There she found a scene of cheerful industry. Goodman was carefully stacking the books on the table, whilst Mrs Castle and her daughter were dusting them and straightening the pages, and Biddy was putting them back on the shelves. As Eve entered the room, Goodman stood up, the last of the fallen books in his hand.

'Oh, thank you,' Eve exclaimed. 'You are so very kind! You cannot imagine how much I was dreading this task!'

'A job's never so bad once you've started it, ma'am,' Mrs Castle replied.

'Biddy, you should still be lying down after your fright,' Eve exclaimed.

'Oh that's all right, ma'am,' said Biddy

stolidly. 'I reckon work's the best medicine.'

'Is M. D'Angers not here?' Eve asked, looking round. 'That's unusual.'

'He sent a message,' Goodman replied. 'His mother's taken a turn for the worse. I'm sorry I wasn't here last night, ma'am,' he went on, contritely. 'I'd have given them what for if I'd been here, I stepped out for some fresh air, thinking that all was secure. How they got in I don't know, for there's no windows broken.'

'Maybe a customer hid and waited until everyone was out of the way,' Eve suggested. 'We must make sure we search the premises before locking up in future. In the meantime, perhaps you would take some wine to M. D'Angers's mother.' She glanced towards the rear of the shop. 'Has anyone looked through there by daylight?'

'Colonel's in there, miss,' Goodman replied.

'Is he indeed?' exclaimed Eve, with a martial tone to her voice that made the others stare.

She walked into the section set aside for the new books with a determined tread. Sure enough, Ballantyne was there, putting some books back on a shelf. He was leaning heavily on a cane.

She stared at his supposedly injured leg.

'Oh, it's back again, is it? I wonder what — '

She was destined not to finish her sentence. Swiftly, he crossed the room, his limp temporarily forgotten, seized hold of her by her shoulders, pulled her against his chest, and kissed her hard on her mouth.

'Colonel Ballantyne!' she exclaimed, as soon as she was able, her face aflame. She opened her mouth to speak.

'One more word from you, and I'll do it again,' he warned in a compelling undertone. 'Now, you're coming with me.'

She shrugged out of his grip. 'I have no desire whatsoever for you to do that again,' she spat at him in a whisper so that those next door would not here. 'But I have yet to understand why I should even go to the end of the street with you, let alone accompany you to some unknown destination.'

'You will accompany me, my dear, because if you refuse to do so, I shall carry you out of this house, informing those in the other room that we have had a lovers' quarrel. I do not think that they would lift a finger to prevent me.'

She could tell by his face that he meant every word. 'Oh, I can well believe it,' she replied in a cynical tone. 'No doubt they are so blinded by your past reputation that they will refuse to believe in your present degeneracy. And you do not need to tell me that the only heed that Mrs Castle would pay would be to warn you to be careful of your leg, because I know it already.'

He gave a shout of laughter. 'Goodman!' he called. 'I am taking Mrs Scorer for a ride after her shock,' he went on, when the man appeared in the doorway. 'Go and tell my groom to have my horses put to, will you?'

'Aye, sir,' Goodman replied.

'I don't suppose he ever executes a sloppy salute,' Eve said crossly when Goodman had gone.

'One of the smartest in the regiment,' Ballantyne replied. 'Shall we go, my dear?'

'I am not your dear, and if you insist that I accompany you, I suppose I shall have to go and put on my bonnet,' she answered with dignity.

He caught hold of her hand and kissed it, before she snatched it away. 'Don't even think about locking yourself in your room,' he warned her. 'I should have absolutely no compunction about breaking your door down, and no difficulty in doing so either.'

She left the room with what was perilously close to being a flounce. She could hear his chuckle as she ascended the stairs. She was tempted to remain upstairs in defiance of the colonel's orders, but decided against it. She had a suspicion that he would do exactly what he had threatened.

'Well, here I am,' she said crossly, on arriving back downstairs. The colonel was now in the library with Goodman, Biddy and Mrs Castle. 'Are we going or not?'

'Charming,' Ballantyne declared, looking her up and down. 'A little outing will soon put you back in a good humour.'

'Indeed it will, sir,' Mrs Castle agreed, beaming. 'You're a real gentleman.'

'He is utterly abominable, infuriating and overbearing,' Eve retorted roundly.

'There you are, then!' responded Mrs Castle, not at all dashed at this description. 'Didn't I tell you how attractive he was to all the ladies?'

Eve greeted this piece of foolishness with a snort of derision.

When Ballantyne had said that he wanted to take her for an outing, Eve had imagined that he would drive her out of the city towards Islington, or perhaps to Bagnigge Wells. In fact, he pointed his horses in the opposite direction, and they were soon driving through busy London streets.

For the first part of the journey, she waited to see whether he would offer any information as to where they might be going. Eventually, consumed by curiosity, she asked him, 'Are we going to the park?'

'No,' he replied. 'I'm taking you to a hotel.'

'What?' she exclaimed, her voice suddenly so loud that one or two passers-by looked up to see who could have spoken thus.

He laughed. 'You are remarkably easy to bait,' he told her. 'Don't be afraid. I'm taking you to meet someone.'

She looked at him doubtfully. 'In a hotel?'

'On my honour,' he replied, his voice and his expression utterly serious this time. Something about his tone made her believe him, even though she told herself that in view of his deceit, it was against all logic.

Eventually, they drew up outside one of the quieter London hotels. A groom hurried to take charge of Ballantyne's horses, and Eve watched while the colonel struggled down painfully, then put out his hand to help her.

'Why must you keep doing that?' she asked him.

'All in good time,' he told her. He put his free hand under her elbow, and she recalled the moment when he had kissed her. She felt a frisson of sensation go right through her.

Without making any enquiries of any of the staff, Ballantyne conducted her up a flight of stairs and along a corridor, passing several doors until he knocked upon one that was almost at the end of the passage. A quietly dressed man who bore the appearance of a valet opened the door.

'Mr Belmont, if you please,' said Ballantyne.

Eve turned quickly to her escort. 'That was the name of the man to whom the bequest would have gone had I refused it,' she said.

'You have a good memory,' the colonel replied. 'Yes, that's so.'

Eve had no time to ask him how he should have known about Belmont, since she certainly had not told him herself, for they were shown into the presence of a thin, quietly dressed man, who was staring out of the window.

'Good morning, Mrs Scorer,' he said in a rather cold, precise voice.

'You aren't Mr Belmont,' said Eve, staring at him. 'You are William Pitt.'

19

'I told you she was intelligent,' said Ballantyne. Then, turning to Eve he asked her, 'Would you like to relinquish your bonnet? We shall be staying for a little while, and I am sure you have plenty of questions that you want to ask.'

'Perhaps I should indeed ask some if I were sure that I would be told the truth,' Eve said in an even tone. 'As it is, I am convinced that I have been shamefully deceived.'

'It was necessary,' Pitt answered. 'Some ratafia, Mrs Scorer?'

Eve accepted, and watched while Ballantyne strode across the room to where glasses and decanters were set on a table against the wall. The power and grace of the man were very evident when he discarded his limp.

'Come, ask us something,' the colonel said, once they were all settled with refreshments. 'Then we will know where to begin.'

'The first thing that I would like to know, is whether my bequest is genuine?' she asked, fearful of the answer. She did not think that she could bear to live on Julia's charity again, should such an unlikely gesture on her cousins part occur.

'Entirely genuine, though a complete surprise to us,' Pitt answered to her relief. 'As far as we were concerned, the property was to have been left to Mr Belmont.'

'Who does not exist, I presume.'

'Who, as you quite rightly surmise, does not exist,' Pitt agreed. 'The name was simply a front for a government agency. Had the business proceeded according to plan, someone given that assumed name would have been placed in the property and from that base would have carried out government work.'

Eve looked at Ballantyne. 'You?' she asked him.

'No, not I,' he answered, shaking his head. 'I'm a serving soldier.'

'Then you have not sold out?'

'No, I have not. But the plan to which Pitt refers was formulated under a very different set of circumstances. For one thing, your relative, Mme Lascelles, was still very much alive, and expected to remain so. The will that she made was only a precaution. For another, I had not sustained an injury which delayed my rejoining my regiment.'

Eve looked puzzled. 'But what had Mme Lascelles to do with your plan? Was she some sort of agent?'

'In a way,' the colonel answered.

'The property has been very valuable to us, because we have known for some time that it has been used by the French as a place to share information,' Pitt told her. 'Madame Lascelles was very adept at pretending to be a sweet, rather muddled old lady who, although residing in England, nevertheless had a weakness for her late husband's country. In fact, her loyalty to England was fierce and her brain very keen indeed. She was fully committed to playing her part in the defeat of Bonaparte.'

'Then why did she decide to leave her property to me?' Eve asked.

'You were her only living relative,' said Pitt. 'We can only assume that sentiment overcame her good judgement at that point. But to continue, shortly before her death, Mme Lascelles sent me documents that were supposed to contain important details of French agents working in this country: their names, their contacts, their plans. These documents were in code, which unfortunately so far has proved to be impossible to break.'

'Did my relative not have any idea of what might be written in the code?' Eve asked.

'She confided one suspicion to me; that there might be a plot to kill the King.'

Eve gasped. 'The King!'

'It's not surprising,' Pitt told her in matter-of-fact tones. 'We've also been trying to get rid of Napoleon. Believe me, our agents are just as busy as theirs. But to return to the matter in hand, one other thing I learned from Mme Lascelles was that there was to be a code book delivered.'

'To the bookshop?' Eve exclaimed. 'Then was that the reason for — '

'For the damage to your shop? Yes, I suspect so,' Ballantyne answered.

'But that doesn't make sense,' Eve said, her brow wrinkling. 'Why did they not ransack the shop before I arrived?'

'Who knows?' Pitt replied, shrugging. 'Perhaps they were not pressed for time, and did not want to arouse suspicion. Perhaps some orders failed to get through.'

Eve still looked puzzled. 'But if the book, or whatever it was, was to be delivered to the shop by French agents, and French agents were expecting it, then why do they suddenly need to start hunting for it?'

'Because Mme Lascelles hid it somewhere before she died, with the intention of passing it on to me.'

'She fell down the stairs before she could do so,' Ballantyne explained, crossing the room with the decanter in order to refill Eve's glass.

'Very inconvenient,' Pitt said calmly, leaning back in his chair and crossing one leg over the other.

'Inconvenient is not the word that I would choose to describe an accident that resulted in someone's death,' Eve said sharply. Neither of the men answered. The colonel had turned away to take the decanter back to the table. Pitt looked at her with the same impassive expression on his face. A dreadful suspicion came into her mind. 'It wasn't an accident, was it?' she said slowly.

'I believe not,' Pitt answered.

'Is it known who was responsible?'

'Regrettably not. So you see, we had a number of reasons for wanting to get one of our people into the shop as soon as possible.'

'So that is why you have been spending so much time at the bookshop,' Eve remarked, looking down into her glass.

'Precisely,' Pitt answered. 'He was there at my orders.'

'Was there ever a real injury?' Eve asked, looking up at the colonel. A cloud of depression was beginning to settle over her, and she could not for the present fathom out why.

'I believe I've already said so,' Ballantyne responded, tight lipped. 'An accident onboard ship as we returned from Egypt meant that I sustained some very painful but comparatively minor injuries.'

'We simply decided to exaggerate the nature of these and pretend that Ballantyne had sold out,' Pitt told her. 'He would thus be free to spend some time in and around the bookshop, to see if he could discover anything about Mme Lascelles' death. In addition he would also make it his business to see if he could find the code book.'

Eve wrinkled her brow. 'Forgive me, but is there not a flaw here?' she said. 'Your aim, surely, is to lull any suspicions that French agents connected with the shop might have. Would not the presence of a former army officer make them very suspicious indeed?'

The colonel opened his mouth to speak, but Pitt forestalled him. 'Not if the said army officer clearly had another reason for visiting the bookshop frequently,' he said, with a thin smile. 'We agreed that if the colonel could deceive people into thinking that he was interested in you, then suspicion would be allayed; especially if he gave the impression that he thought that the war was over for good.'

'In short, sirs, you have made use of me,' Eve said, rather pleased to discover that her voice did not wobble as she spoke. The suspicion that the colonel had only been thinking of her as a means to an end had been dawning upon her throughout this conversation, but to hear it put into words was more painful than she would have expected.

'No, madam, England has made use of you,' Pitt answered coldly, 'as indeed she has made use of all of us. Do you begrudge your country this small service in time of need?'

'I must apologize — ' the colonel began.

'Pray do not, sir. I understand perfectly,' Eve answered in an airy tone, cutting him off. 'What is a little flirtation in comparison with the safety of the realm? At least now I know why you were pretending to limp.'

'That was why I had to bring you here today,' Ballantyne told her. 'I could not risk your revealing the truth to anyone.'

'Except for Goodman and Mrs Castle, I suppose,' Eve surmised.

'Their advent was pure coincidence, although strangely enough, I did write a recommendation for Goodman, which found its way into your solicitor's hands. Since then, he has been informed about a small part of this. Mrs Castle is no wiser than you were before you came here today.'

'I see,' said Eve. Silence fell upon the whole room. Eventually Eve spoke again. 'Now that all of that has been settled, may I go home?'

'Presently,' said Pitt. 'Before you do so, however, it is important to establish what you are going to do with the information that you have learned today.'

She stared at him indignantly. 'Naturally, I will keep this information to myself,' she replied haughtily. 'I will do what I can to look for the code book. Colonel Ballantyne', and here she tried very hard not to grit her teeth, 'will be welcome, of course, as a regular customer.'

'I must insist that you make him a little more welcome than that,' Pitt said. 'The fact that it was deemed necessary to turn your premises upside down so that the code book could be discovered indicates that those responsible are becoming more desperate. This means that we, in our turn, need to regard its discovery as a matter of urgency.'

'In that case, I will personally hunt for it as soon as I get home,' said Eve crisply. 'There is no need to trouble the colonel.'

'You are not thinking clearly,' Ballantyne told her. 'Those who are hunting for this code book are almost certainly the same people who killed Mme Lascelles. They will undoubtedly deal similarly with anyone who gets in their way. You will not be safe until these people are caught.'

'My son,' Eve faltered. She felt Ballantyne

grip her shoulder. Then she went on in a firmer tone, 'The solution is quite simple. I have to think of my son's safety first. I will just go into the country and leave the bookshop in the hands of Mr Belmont until this matter is concluded.'

'That won't do, I fear,' said Ballantyne. 'Unfortunately, you may now be suspected of being part of our own spy network. Away from London we cannot guarantee your safety.'

'More importantly, moving you out and moving someone else in would lose us valuable time, and divert attention from the task in hand,' put in Pitt. 'No, Mrs Scorer, I fear that there is only one solution to the problem, which will at one and the same time keep you protected, and enable us to make the necessary search. You will have to take Ballantyne for your lover.'

For a moment, Eve felt as if all the breath had been knocked out of her. 'I beg your pardon?' she said faintly as soon as she was able. 'I do not think I can have heard you correctly.'

'My God, Pitt, you go too far,' Ballantyne protested. His colour was heightened and he looked just as shocked as Eve.

'It's the perfect solution,' said Pitt, quite unmoved by the reactions of the two people in front of him. 'It will enable you, Ballantyne, to stay overnight in Clerkenwell Green. This will at one and the same time provide Mrs Scorer with a bodyguard, and also give you the opportunity of searching the premises at your leisure. If you play your parts well, our adversaries may be convinced that you are simply wrapped up in one another, and oblivious to anything that may be going on around you.'

'I won't do it. It's monstrous to expect it of . . . of Mrs Scorer,' declared Ballantyne.

'I don't know why you're so squeamish all of a sudden,' Pitt protested. 'You were quite willing to seduce her when I first suggested it to you.'

'Damn it all!' Ballantyne exploded, walking across to the table in order to refill his glass.

'Well, Mrs Scorer?' Pitt asked. 'Are you prepared to take Ballantyne as your lover for the sake of your country?'

Eve stood up, straightening her shoulders. 'No, sir, I am not,' she said frankly. 'I am, however, prepared to consider allowing such a deceit to be practised for the sake of my country, so that these scoundrels may be caught. My willingness even to think about the matter will depend on two conditions.'

'And what will those be, ma'am?' Pitt asked, also standing. Ballantyne was still at the table, leaning on it with both his hands. His back was turned towards them.

'The first will be that you write down exactly what I have agreed to and why, together with the information that this . . . liaison between the colonel and myself is false. Should any rumours reach my son's ears in time to come, I would like to be in a position to discredit them so that he will not lose faith in his mother's honour. The second is that Colonel Ballantyne will not use his position to take advantage of me.'

'Agreed,' said Pitt.

Eve held up her hand. 'Forgive me, sir, but the granting of the second is beyond your powers. Colonel Ballantyne began this whole affair ready to seduce me. I need to have his word of honour on this — if, indeed, honour, and a willingness to seduce innocent females, can ever be said to go together.'

The colonel turned then. He stood upright, his face set as if it were carved from granite. 'I'll never force myself upon you,' he told her in clipped accents. 'You have my word.'

'You must think quickly, madam,' said Pitt. 'Time is of the essence here.'

After that, there was very little more to be said. The colonel and the statesman exchanged more conversation whilst Eve looked about her at the room which, truth to tell, had about as much character as any hotel room might have been expected to have. She forced herself to display an interest in her surroundings, however. It was either that, or give way to the conflicting thoughts and emotions that were tearing at her at the present time.

There was a picture hanging over the mantelpiece depicting some Greek hero arriving in Athens in triumph. Would she have any triumphs to recall when she left London, Eve asked herself? Triumph in this new role would, at best, mean safety for the King, and the unmasking of a number of enemy agents. She supposed she ought to be proud of that.

Colonel Ballantyne's voice recalled her from her reverie. 'Mrs Scorer, are you ready to go?'

'Yes, thank you, Colonel Ballantyne.'

'Rather formal for lovers,' Pitt observed.

'That has not yet been agreed,' Eve reminded him.

'Think of your country, madam,' he replied coldly. 'Don't forget your stick, Ballantyne.'

'Or your limp,' Eve added tartly, as she swept out of the room.

They maintained a rather frosty silence until they were once more in the colonel's curricle, and Jason said 'Eve, we need to talk.'

'Mrs Scorer to you.'

'Mrs Scorer, then.'

'What makes you think that I want to exchange a single syllable with you?' Eve asked sweetly.

'For God's sake, don't be so foolish,' he snapped impatiently, if not very wisely.

'Oh, I'm foolish now, am I? Well, since I was simple enough to be an easy target for seduction, I suppose I must be. *You* may need to talk, but I do not have the patience or the inclination to listen to you at the moment. Kindly take me home.'

The colonel gave a sigh of exasperation, Eve put up her parasol so as to obscure her view of him entirely, and they completed their journey to Clerkenwell Green in tense silence.

'May I call upon you in a day or two — when you have had chance to . . . ' — he was going to say 'to cool down' but after pausing completed his sentence perhaps more wisely with ' . . . to reflect on things.'

'I suppose you had better,' she replied. With that he had to be content.

★   ★   ★

Over the next day or two, Eve kept her uncharitable thoughts about the colonel at bay by trying to keep herself busy. Part of her wanted to close the bookshop, but she knew

313

that this would be unwise. Apart from anything else, maintaining it would give her something else to think about other than the colonel's deceit. She was annoyed with the way in which she had been used, but she was a patriotic Englishwoman, and liked to think that she might be able to do her bit towards trapping a French agent. Of her growing regard for Ballantyne she refused to think.

Furthermore, if she did not open the shop, what would she do? She could, of course, spend more time with Luke, but Miss Sparrow, who seemed to be glad of any excuse to avoid visiting her sister, was enjoying educating the little boy. She did not want to disrupt his routine, which was working well.

She had a number of visitors to the shop, but none of them looked particularly like a French spy. There was only one disturbing incident. This took place when Mr Harpin and M. Monceux came to the shop one day. During this incident, Monceux had been very conversable, whilst Harpin spent a lot of time examining the contents of the bookshelves. They had left without purchasing anything.

She had to attend to them herself, since M. D'Angers's mother was still unwell, and she had sent Biddy Todd to help them — not without vigorous protests on Biddy's part.

'You've had a nasty shock,' Eve insisted. 'It'll do you good to get out of the house.'

Even with the shop to attend to, Eve still had a little time to think where her relative might have hidden the code book. If she had been Mme Lascelles, where would she have put it? Would it make sense to hide it here in the shop, or upstairs in the living quarters? If enemy agents wanted to leave messages, then a bookshop or a library would be a good place. If the person who wanted to conceal something was the occupant of the premises, however, would it not make more sense to hide the item upstairs, where not so many people would come?

She tried to conduct an unobtrusive search of all the upstairs rooms. This was not very easy. She did not want anyone to see what she was doing because she did not want such activities noticed and remarked upon, in all innocence, perhaps even in front of an enemy agent.

The rooms had still had a lot of Mme Lascelles's knick-knacks about when she had arrived, so searching was no easy matter. When eventually the colonel did arrive to take her out in his curricle, she was satisfied that she had made as thorough a search as she was capable of, but with no results.

'Where are you taking me?' she asked him.

'To Berkeley Square,' he told her. 'My mother and cousin are out, and there's less chance of listening ears than at your establishment.' She was about to refute this indignantly, but realized in time how absurd this would sound under the circumstances and held her peace.

Servants hurried out to help them both down on their arrival, and to take charge of the curricle. Eve turned to watch Ballantyne being assisted to alight. She now saw the grim set to his mouth quite differently. Before, she had put such expressions down to pain, and impatience with his disability. Now she realized that his anger must be because he longed to be able to spring down athletically, as he was clearly quite capable of doing. To her great surprise, she felt a rush of sympathy for him.

'Wine, to the drawing room if you please,' he said to the butler, then conducted Eve to the room where she had met Mrs Ballantyne and Miss Mirfield when she had dined there. Again, silence fell until the wine had been brought.

Once they were unobserved, he walked easily from the side table with two glasses in his hand. 'What are you thinking about?' Ballantyne asked her.

'Now?'

'Mm.'

'Oh.' She looked down into her wine. 'I was thinking about how vexing it must be for you to have to move in that halting way, when you are obviously so . . . so . . . ' She paused, blushing.

'So?' he raised his brows.

'So athletic,' she concluded, not looking directly at him.

'It is damned vexing,' he agreed, 'but that isn't the worst of it.'

'What *is* the worst of it?' she asked curiously.

'The deceit,' he replied. She snorted with derision. 'Oh, you think that's amusing, do you?' he demanded. 'What do you think I am? I'm a soldier, Eve, a soldier. I meet the enemy face to face, out in the open, with a uniform on my body and a sword in my hand. When Pitt summoned me and asked me to take on this piece of work, I agreed because I wanted to do my duty, but the idea of sneaking about and taking part in subterfuge gave me no pleasure. Apart from anything else, I don't think I'm very good at it.'

'Mr Pitt said that you were going to seduce me, and you did not deny it,' she said accusingly.

'I was prepared to go to such lengths,' he admitted, 'but that was before I knew you.'

'Oh, so it's all right to seduce women as long as one doesn't know them,' she exclaimed ironically.

'That isn't what I meant and you know damn' well it isn't,' he declared angrily.

'What did you mean, then?'

He ran his hand impatiently through his hair. 'I don't know,' he confessed. 'Perhaps the whole business didn't seem real before I met you.'

'Why did you not tell me all about it?' Eve asked. 'I think that your lack of candour is one of the things that I am finding it hardest to forgive. In any case, had I known about what you were doing, I could perhaps have helped in some way.'

Ballantyne shook his head. 'I could not take the risk,' he said. 'I had no way of knowing how much you might give away. A comment let slip by you in all innocence could have put someone on their guard.'

Eve remembered how she had had that very thought when she was trying to search her house for signs of the code book. 'Then in the end, you were the one who gave the game away,' she remarked.

'I told you that I was no good at subterfuge. Besides, I think you'll have to acknowledge that I've found out very little. Speaking of which, what are we to do about Pitt's latest plan?'

close. 'I think that the sooner the government buys this shop from you the better.'

'Will they still need someone to manage the shop?' Eve asked him. 'I should hate to feel that M. D'Angers was to be cast off without means of supporting himself and his mother.'

'I'll speak up for him,' Jason told her. 'It will be my business to make sure that you have no excuse for putting off our wedding. I want you thoroughly tied to me in bonds of matrimony before war breaks out again.'

'I have no intention of escaping,' she said demurely. 'Is this what it means when they say that someone is under military arrest?'

'In a manner of speaking,' he answered, tipping her back and kissing her until she was breathless.

'With such masterful tactics, you will surely be a general one day,' she replied, as soon as she was able.

'You're not disappointed that I haven't sold out?'

'I know that's the life you have chosen and I love and honour you for it. What's more, Luke is delighted that you will still be Colonel Blazes.' Eve had been cautious about telling Luke that she was to be married again, but the little boy had been overjoyed to hear that his mama was to marry his hero.

'It sounds better than Mr Blazes, doesn't it?'

'Much better,' Eve replied.

'And I hope you think that even Mr Blazes sounds better than Mr Bunty.'

At this point a small tussle ensued, as Eve attempted to escape from the colonel's clutches, and the colonel applied his strength and ingenuity to preventing her from doing so. Given his superior power, the result was a foregone conclusion, but the struggle provided a few moments' highly agreeable amusement for the parties concerned.

'I was never interested in Mr Bunty, as you very well know,' said Eve in an indignant tone which was rather robbed of its superior nature by the dishevelled state of her hair. 'Where Julia was concerned, however — '

'And *I* was never interested in Mrs Comberton, as *you* very well know,' the colonel interrupted.

'I can't imagine why not,' said Eve candidly. 'She is exceedingly pretty, and *she* was very interested in *you*.'

'I can only speak for myself, but in my opinion, a woman's prettiness rapidly disappears when her claws come out,' answered the colonel frankly. 'I dislike predatory females. The one female whom I adore is gallant and loyal and loving, and altogether more desirable than this inarticulate soldier can possibly express.'

'This inarticulate soldier is doing very well,' replied Eve, rewarding him with a kiss.

'I've spoken to Pitt, and he has agreed that the government will purchase the shop from you at a fair price. Then you can concentrate on being the colonel's lady.'

'I shall love being the colonel's lady,' she replied, returning his embrace with enthusiasm, and so she did until the day when, to her great relief, following the Battle of Waterloo, General Sir Jason Ballantyne returned safely to his home, his children and her arms, covered with glory.

We do hope that you have enjoyed reading this large print book.

Did you know that all of our titles are available for purchase?

We publish a wide range of high quality large print books including:
Romances, Mysteries, Classics
General Fiction
Non Fiction and Westerns

Special interest titles available in large print are:
The Little Oxford Dictionary
Music Book
Song Book
Hymn Book
Service Book

Also available from us courtesy of Oxford University Press:
Young Readers' Dictionary
(large print edition)
Young Readers' Thesaurus
(large print edition)

For further information or a free brochure, please contact us at:
Ulverscroft Large Print Books Ltd.,
The Green, Bradgate Road, Anstey,
Leicester, LE7 7FU, England.
Tel: (00 44) 0116 236 4325
Fax: (00 44) 0116 234 0205

Other titles published by
The House of Ulverscroft:

LADY OF LINCOLN

Ann Barker

For Emily Whittaker living in Lincoln, the closest thing to romance is her lukewarm relationship with Dr Boyle. But a new friendship with Nathalie Fanshawe brings interest to her life. Then Canon Trimmer and his family move into the cathedral close. When Mrs Trimmer's brother, Sir Gareth Blades visits them, he seems a romantic figure, and apparently attracted to Emily. But she finds a mysterious side to Sir Gareth with the arrival of Annis Hughes, not to mention his connection with Mrs Fanshawe . . . Is Sir Gareth really a gallant gentleman or would Emily be better off settling for Dr Boyle after all?

THE OTHER MISS FROBISHER

Ann Barker

Elfrida Frobisher leaves her country backwater and her suitor to chaperon Prudence, her eighteen-year-old niece, in London. Unfortunately, Prudence has apparently developed an attachment for an unsuitable man, which she fosters behind her aunt's back. Attempting to foil her niece's schemes and prevent a scandal, Elfrida only succeeds in finding herself involved with the eligible Rufus Tyler in a scandal of her own! Fleeing London seems the only solution — but Prudence has another plan . . . Elfrida yearns for her quiet rural existence, but it takes a mad dash in pursuit of her niece before she realises where her heart truly lies.